ANGEL EYES

Also by Robert Dietrich

The Steve Bentley Thrillers

Murder on the Rocks
End of a Stripper
The House on Q Street
Mistress to Murder
Murder on Her Mind
Angel Eyes
Curtains for a Lover
Calypso Caper
Curtains for a Lover
My Body
Guilty Knowledge

ANGEL EYES

ROBERT DIETRICH

CUTTING EDGE

ISBN-13:

Published by
Cutting Edge Publishing
PO Box 8212
Calabasas, CA 91372

CHAPTER ONE

She was leaning against the frame of the partly open doorway, eying me sulkily. A bobbed ash blonde in a translucent black silk nightgown ending at the knees. Her legs and feet were bare. Even the hallway's semilight couldn't conceal the sleek, sexy figure. The face was a young face with a minx expression, high cheekbones and overmuch lipstick. I was fitting my key in my door when she spoke: "He didn't come."

She said it listlessly, slightly slurring the words. Her right hand strayed from the doorknob and rubbed her chin. "The bastard," she went on dully. "The Great Lover. At least he coulda let me know." Her body shifted slightly and she peered at me.

"That's a man for you," I murmured and pushed my door inward. "The hell with them all."

Her head cocked and her eyes opened wide. She wasn't totally shellacked. Not yet. But she had been plucking the booze bush long enough to get heavily relaxed. My new next-door neighbor, a nearly nude ash blonde lovely, and playful as a week-old kitten.

"Hey," she called. "What's the big hurry?"

Stopping, I turned and shrugged. "End of a hard day. That and long habit."

She took a deep breath and pushed herself away from the door frame. "How come I never saw you before?"

"I've been away. When'd you move in, neighbor?"

"Last week. Where'd you go?"

"The Virgin Islands."

Her head tilted back and she laughed throatily. Then she looked at me with raised eyebrows. "Don't tell me there's still enough around to stock a whole goddam island?"

"Maybe it's just a name."

She nodded thoughtfully. Then she tilted her head provocatively and purred, "I'm Peachy."

"What I can see from here is sensational."

Her nose wrinkled. "I mean my name, you. Peachy. Peachy Bolac."

"Steve Bentley."

"I know. I read your name card. Want a drink, Steve?"

"That's real neighborly," I mused. "I might just accept a dram of chuckleberry cordial."

"Whatever that is."

"Or anything else you might have handy. Tell you what, I'll change my shirt and slide over. Say ten minutes."

"The door'll be open." She drifted back inside and I went into my apartment.

Dropping my briefcase on a table I pulled off my coat and tie, wondering who had stood up Peachy Bolac and if she customarily received male visitors so negligibly clad. The apartment management was conservative enough not to go for call girl setups or backstairs wives, but a week's residence wouldn't be conclusive either way. As I stepped into the shower I told myself a drink and a chat with the new neighbor might be just what I needed. I had gone through a long afternoon session at Tax Court and a change of pace might be a good idea before tackling the tax work I had brought home. In any case, I argued, I would be mixing a drink for myself before dinner; why not take advantage of Peachy's hospitality?

Within the specified time I had shaved, gotten into loafers, slacks and a sport shirt, and when I closed her door behind me I saw her half lying in the corner of a sofa, eyes closed.

The apartment layout was the same as mine: living room, dining room, two bedrooms and kitchen. Her furniture was new,

Williamsburg replica with petit-point seat covers and matching Colonial draperies. One lighted table lamp gave a soft yellow glow and from where I stood I could scan considerable milk-white thigh. A peaceful scene, easy on the eyes and nerves. I whistled and her eyes opened. She started, sat up and said, "Oh!" Then she brushed back hair from her forehead with her right hand. Blinking, she fussed down the hem of her nightgown and said, "Scotch's over there. I'll take bourbon."

"With or without?"

"Just ice."

I built a couple of drinks, stuck a cigarette in my jaw and walked over to the sofa. She was sitting there as demurely as a wallflower, staring up at me, knees together, black silk pulled tautly across her thighs. Her left wrist sported a thin gold bracelet, no rings on her fingers. Handing her the bourbon highball, I said, "Welcome to Washington."

She sipped and frowned. "You live here long?"

"About four years in this building. In Washington most of my life."

"It's a lousy town," she said petulantly. "I hate its lousy guts."

I sat down beside her and hung one leg across the other. "It's a great city," I said. "All you need is money, endurance and powerful friends. But in a pinch money alone will do."

"Yeah. What's your racket?"

"Racket? I'm a C.P.A."

She eyed me for what seemed like a long time. "You sure don't look it, brother," she said flatly.

"What's a C.P.A. supposed to look like? Honest Bob Cratchit, all hunched-over and myopic from toil?"

She giggled suddenly. "I read about him once. The *Christmas Carol*. By Robert Louis Stevenson." Her voice was triumphant.

"Say, you've been to school," I observed. "And Dickens wrote *Treasure Island,* my favorite book. How time slips by."

Her glass clinked against mine. "Merry Christmas, Steve." She giggled again. A practiced giggler. Abruptly she leaned forward and reached for my cigarette. Her cheeks hollowed, she inhaled and fumbled the cigarette back into my fingers. She angled back against the arm of the sofa and stared up at the ceiling. Smoke drifted lazily upward. She seemed to have forgotten about me. About anything at all. Smoke climbed toward the shadowed ceiling. I sipped my drink and studied her. The troublesome silken hem had done some climbing of its own. Another couple of inches and there would be no secrets between us. I cleared my throat modestly.

Slowly, spitefully she said, "The dirty bastard!"

"Dickens?"

Her head tossed. "No, not him. Tom … I mean …" She sat upright and brushed down the negligent hem.

"Tom who?"

"Never mind," she said guiltily.

"The guy who didn't drop around. Yes?"

"I'll show him he can't keep me sitting around here just waiting for him. He can't go on treating me like I was only a cheap lay, the bastard!"

"Especially on Christmas. On the other hand this being July, maybe Tom just forgot."

Her eyes turned and studied me. Large dark eyes, nearly round and veiled. "Look," she said finally, "forget that. I didn't say anybody's name. Okay?"

"Okay, Angel Eyes."

That brought a smile to her lips. She leaned back, her tongue flicked across her glass and she said cozily, "You're not a bad guy."

"As neighbors go. I take it you're not married?"

She laughed harshly. "Peachy married? Peachy's not the marrying kind." Then she seemed to slump and her face held the look of a lost and frightened child.

I got up, went over to the radio and found a record program on WTOP. When I came back her glass was empty. She held it out to me and I made another highball. On the light side. When I fitted the glass into her hand her mouth was slack, her eyes remote and her arm weaved uncertainly. A couple more of the same and Peachy Bolac would need no Nembutal to sleep the night through.

Butting my cigarette, I felt for another when she swayed against me and planted a wet kiss near my mouth. Giggling, she tilted her chin and said, "I like you, Steve."

"Well," I said, "I like you, too. It's nice we're neighbors."

She nodded agreement. "But you mustn't come here just *any* time. I'll let you know when you can come. Okay?"

"Fine as wine. But why the secrecy?"

Her forehead furrowed. "Well—*he* wouldn't like it. He might—"

"My heart's in my mouth."

"Oh, *you* ..." Her lips pursed and she leaned forward again to be kissed. I obliged.

They were full lips, dark as oxblood cherries, and damply hot. I put down my drink and removed hers. That brought her over across my lap. God knows where the hem was fluttering. She rubbed against me catlike, moaning a little and her teeth nibbled the end of my tongue. Somehow one full breast nestled into the cup of my right hand. Between us there was nothing but two ounces of black silk. Tough luck, Tom, I thought, but youth will be served. Her eyes closed. Suddenly her body sagged and went slack. The arm that had been behind my head fell limply away and her breathing grew calm and regular. Peachy Bolac had passed out.

Grating my teeth, I slid out from under her, laid her head down on a pillow and lifted her legs, arranging the nightgown modestly. Angel Eyes had rocketed off somewhere around the far side of the moon leaving me alone and restless. Straightening up,

I muttered, "You're hell with the ladies, Bentley," drained the rest of my drink and put down the empty glass. Turning, I surveyed what the single lamp showed of the room. It was as impersonal as a hot-sheet motel. All except for a photograph in a leather frame on the table beside the lamp. Walking toward it, I saw a man's jowly face surmounted by stagy white hair. Around the wattled neck hung a starched collar and a black string tie. I didn't need to read the scrawled dedication to know who had written it, who Peachy had been waiting for. Who Tom was. He would be Senator Tom Quinby. Sixty-four if he was a day, from a backwoods, hillbilly state that featured razorback hawgs, turkey-neck sharecroppers and contempt for Civil Rights. A florid, shirtsleeve orator of the William Jennings Bryan school. A prohibitionist and a flag-waving moralizer. I picked up the picture and chuckled. "You old lecher," I murmured. "Imagine finding you here." Then I put it down and looked back at Peachy.

One arm was flung aside, a knee had flexed slightly. She was only in her mid-twenties but sleep had erased ten years from her face. I had a paternal urge to draw a coverlet over her but it was a hot night in Washington, and passed-out she might smother. So I turned and walked toward the door.

Just then the buzzer sounded.

CHAPTER TWO

The sound froze me. I stared at the shadowed door and swore silently. Then I realized Senator Quinby would also have some explaining to do so I sucked a deep breath and went the rest of the way. Gripping the knob I glanced back at Peachy. Her face was shadowed by the end of the sofa but her white legs were clearly visible. Facing around, I opened the door a crack.

No Senator Quinby. No Bible-belt hawg-caller with pompadoured white hair and a linen duster. Not even a man.

I was looking at a woman in a tailored turquoise suit, matching gloves and a feathery wisp of a hat. The gloves were in one hand and she was tapping them against her other thumb. Instead of tapping her foot—she was that well bred. Her dark penciled eyebrows lifted in mild surprise, the soft tapping of her gloves stopped and she frowned slightly. A rather haughty accent said, "I'm sorry—I rather thought Miss Bolac lived here."

"So she does."

The caller had too much poise to blink. Instead she gazed past me and said archly, "I may have come at an inopportune moment. Would you be good enough to tell Miss Bolac that Alma Ward would like to speak with her?"

"I'm sorry, Miss Ward. Peachy isn't receiving folks just now."

The bosom lifted, the voice shifted range and took on a harmonic of sharpness. "I don't believe you. Tell her I'm here. And I don't like waiting."

"A thousand pardons, dear lady. Believe me, no commonplace fellow like myself would intentionally obstruct a person of your importance, but it so happens that Miss Bolac isn't receiving this evening. At the moment she isn't even conscious."

Her hands went to her hips and I heard a defiant snort. "You won't mind if I verify that?"

I let her push the door open and step past me. She went all the way to the sofa, stopped and picked up Peachy's arm, then let it drop. Pivoting, she faced me. "Drunk, I suppose," she said scornfully.

"Good God, what an idea!"

She took two steps toward me and stopped. "I don't particularly like impudence, either, but I suppose you'd be the boy friend—I believe that's the phrase."

"As the riffraff have it. We were just about to show colored slides. I happen to be a neighbor."

She laughed unpleasantly. "How convenient for you both." Then she walked past me to the door, half turned and surveyed the room. "So entirely in keeping," she said loftily. "A cheap little apartment for a cheap little tramp. If you're staying around—and I don't for a minute doubt her allure—you might remember to tell her I stopped by. And add that our business won't keep forever."

I bowed from the hips. "I'm terribly impressed, Miss Ward, and I'll do my best to keep your message straight. But if I happen to get things a trifle confused it'll be because it's not every day I get walked over by a lady as generally attractive as you."

Whirling, she strode out into the hall. I grinned and glanced back at the girl on the sofa. "Angel Eyes," I said, "you have the damnedest friends."

Her face nuzzled the pillow as though part of what I said had pierced the barrier of time and space, but if it had it faded as quickly. Only the rhythmic lifting of her lovely breasts told me that she was still part of the earth.

As I opened my apartment door again I remembered Alma Ward's hauteur. Hell, with her dough, she could afford it. Her father had been an old pirate who built and ran a newspaper empire, reduced after his death to one Washington and two Maryland dailies. Alma had been born to the sound of golden chimes, then schools in France and Switzerland, honors at Bennington, a couple of years covering the White House for one of the family rags, and finally her own TV program: *Washington Scene.* One of those Sunday afternoon quiz and yawn panels, heavy on Prime Ministers, Undersecretaries, Cabinet members and influential Congressmen. Big deal. I walked to the bar, built another drink, feather-light on the soda, and stared at it sourly. It was none of my business who paid Peachy Bolac's rent, less what she and Alma Ward meant to each other. I rated no applause for the way I had let Alma Ward push me around, but on the other hand the setting was a poor one for a pitched battle. I should figure myself lucky for being back in my own digs with no nail marks in my skin. From time to time I had glimpsed Alma Ward's handsomely aristocratic features on the big tube and wondered, like a lot of males, if her stainless steel exterior was solid all the way. The recent close-up suggested that it was.

My wristwatch marked eight-fifteen. I could thaw some food in the oven or I could drive down to Arbaugh's for ribs and beer. The latter sounded like the better idea so I went into the bedroom for a coat. While I was pulling it on I could hear the buzzer sound in Peachy's apartment. The sound came through the wall faintly and insistently. At first I thought Senator Quinby had arrived, but as I walked into the living room I realized that he would have his own key. Putting my wallet in my coat pocket, I scooped up cigarettes and a lighter and went out into the hall.

Next door a man was pressing Peachy's button. A man about five-ten with dark eyebrows, a deep tan and crewcut black hair. He wore a navy blue summer suit, black shoes and a gold wristwatch. A man in his early thirties. He could have been hockey coach at a good Eastern prep school. At the sound of my door closing he turned and glanced at me. Then he stepped back from the door, looked at it and said, "Happen to know if there's anyone home?"

"The apartment's been vacant for some time. Sure your party's the tenant?"

He nodded and grimaced. "Positive."

"Might ask at the desk."

"I did. Key's gone. They said she was up here. She made a call about an hour ago through the switchboard."

"A lot can happen in an hour," I said. "Empires can fall. I'd leave a card and try tomorrow."

"Thanks," he said crisply and felt for his wallet. As I walked past him I saw him fishing for a card. Tough luck, laddie, I thought. You came too early or too late. Depending on what you came for.

I rode the elevator down to the garage, got into my still-hot Olds and shot up the ramp to the street. Once on Massachusetts I angled over Calvert to Connecticut and found a few yards of spare curb not too far from Arbaugh's. Walking into Arbaugh's, I tried to figure out why Peachy's male caller looked familiar to me. I had seen that frank, darkly handsome face before but the connection didn't come to me. Sinking into a booth, I ordered smoked ribs and a stein of musty ale. Both reached me in record time and as I started in I realized that I had been hungry for a long time. After the ribs I drank another stein and ordered pie à la mode and coffee. Driving back to the apartment I managed to put Peachy and her callers out of my mind long enough to organize my waiting tax work, and by the time I was strolling down the corridor I was primed to work until midnight.

As I passed Peachy's door I noticed a calling card stuck between the door and the frame. Halting, I pulled it out and read it. It was an ordinary white card, printed, not engraved with a man's name: *Jay Redpath*. That would be the tanned man. Below and in smaller type: *Special Counsel Joint Congressional Committee on Legislative Oversight*. The catchall Committee that investigated anything overlooked by the multitude of other Congressional Committees. I turned the card over and saw a scrawled telephone number. Then I flicked the card with my thumbnail and frowned. If I stuck it back where it had been Peachy could peek out for a breath of fresh air and miss it. If Senator Quinby stopped by it would be there for him to see and wonder about. Either alternative seemed unsatisfactory so I dropped the card in my pocket. In the morning I would hand it to her or leave it in her box downstairs. It seemed the least I could do—for a neighbor.

Inside my apartment I turned on the Ampex stereo and fitted a new Les Baxter tape on the spindle. Adjusting the volume low, I opened my briefcase and spread my papers on the table. Then I sat down and got to work. Five cigarettes later I got up, stretched and perked some coffee. I watched late TV long enough to drink two cups black, then I switched it off, laid a new tape reel on the Ampex and went back to work.

By midnight I was red-eyed and groggy. Turning off the lamp, I went into the kitchen, drank a glass of milk and got into bed. Between the coffee and the problems threading through my mind I was too wound up to sleep. Instead I tossed like an apprentice yogi on a spike mattress, and something after three I got up, pulled on pants and a shirt and stalked out for a stroll around the block.

The corridor lights were low but not so low that I couldn't notice Peachy's door partly open as I passed. Slowing, I stopped and went back. Peering through the doorway, I saw that the living room was darker than the Tunnel of Love. The lamp I had left on had been turned off. "Hello," I called. "Anybody home?"

No answer.

What I should have done was close the door quietly and go my way. What I did was step back, consider the situation and press the buzzer. It sounded somewhere in the dark apartment, a harsh, lonely sound. I rang it again. I didn't like to think of her lying there in the darkness, probably still passed out, with the door open. I listened for the sound of the elevator, heard none, and stepped inside.

Through the darkness I found my way to the table lamp, fumbled for the switch and pressed it. A radius of yellow light spread out from the table. Blinking, I turned and faced the sofa. The pillow was there but nothing else. No Peachy. In bed probably. She had wakened, still woozy, opened the door and staggered off to bed for the rest of the night.

Before we had started chewing each other I had placed her highball on the carpet. The glass lay on its side, the liquor was a dark blob where it had flowed away. Well, she could have knocked it over when she sat up. I shook out a cigarette, lighted it and made up my mind. Leaving the table, I went to the door and closed it gently. Then I crossed the room and went down the hall that led to the bedrooms. No lights there, either. Nothing. I switched on the hall light and saw one open bedroom door. Walking to it, I reached around and turned on the light. All I had intended to do was flash it quickly to satisfy myself that she was asleep and well. Then I would leave.

What I saw made me grab the door frame and gasp.

She was on the bed, all right, naked and with one leg drawn up and twisted underneath her other thigh. Her eyes stared vacantly at the ceiling light. Her hands were tied behind her back, I couldn't see with what. But her mouth was bound and gagged with a knotted silk stocking. Its mate was drawn brutally tight around her neck and knotted under the angle of her jaw. Her face was cyanosed and puffy. Rigor or the tightness of the gag had curled her upper lip nearly to her nostrils. I didn't have to listen to her heart or touch her skin to know that she was dead. Even if it was passionately formed in life a dead female body is nothing to leer at and make you lick your lips. Dead it's only so much chill butchered meat. Turning, I fought for breath and walked back into the living room.

My staring eyes noticed something that made me stop. Something was out of place. No, missing. I edged toward the lamp table and studied it. The photograph. Not there any longer. Removed by Peachy, maybe, but more probably by the killer. A lot more likely by him.

I opened the door, left it ajar and went into my apartment. Before I went to the phone I picked up a fifth, pulled the cork and drank. Cold out of the bottle the liquor tasted like the edge of a knife. Then I dialed Police Headquarters.

When the bored Sergeant's voice answered, I said, "Give me Captain Kellaway, Homicide."

CHAPTER THREE

Ten years before Pearl Harbor the office walls had been painted cream. Now they were streaked with soot and flaking. Where the paint peeled it left light outlines as jagged as a Dow-Jones stock chart. I was sitting in a chair beside a scarred walnut-veneer desk. There was a worn carpet on the stone floor and two battered gooseneck lamps on the desk. The desk held a pile of dog-eared folders and a rubble of tarnished cartridges, brass shells, fully used strip blotters, a rusty stapler, and a dip pen-set with a faded lumber ad along the pen barrel. Against the wall a grimy tilt-glass bookcase held books with undecipherable titles. They would be on criminology and forensic law, police organization and the like. The office belonged to Captain Kellaway, Homicide, Metropolitan Police. Kellaway sat behind the desk writing methodically. He had been writing for the last ten minutes. It seemed he had forgotten I was there.

I turned my head enough to look at the open Venetian blinds. Below them on a covered radiator stood an oval emerald-green bowl. It was Japanese and it held a dwarf Japanese tree banked in velvety moss. Kellaway had told me once what it was. Chinese juniper or ginger or something on that order. He had mentioned it a long time ago and I hadn't kept it well in mind. *Bonsai* was his hobby, not mine. I flipped a butt in a shiny spittoon—the only polished article in the place—and fitted a new gasper between my teeth. I was ready to do some more waiting. With the cops, your time is their time.

Sooner than I expected Kellaway laid aside his ball pen and peered at me.

I said, "I liked the other one better."

"The other *what?*"

"The office you had when you were just a Lootenant. Noisy, yes, even on the bustly side, but sunlight entered and if it smelled of anything it was coffee and dime cigars, not must and mold. Or maybe this is the price you pay for success."

"Could be," Kellaway said irritably. "Anyway, this is what I got now, like it or not. Since it offends you so much, some Saturday when you're not off sailing you could roll up your sleeves and help me paint the place. I suppose you'd like passionate pink?"

"Pansy purple will do."

Kellaway pulled out a large handkerchief and wiped his face. Somewhere in the background the air-conditioner was pumping, but it might as well have been in San Francisco. He swigged the dregs of a paper coffee container and dropped it into the waste basket. Then he swiveled around and faced me.

"She was raped," he said roughly.

I said nothing.

He said, "Tell me you're surprised, Steve."

I shrugged. "Alive she was one hell of a succulent dish. By eight last night she was stoned. I told you how she was hanging out of her door feeling surly and go-to-hell. And in the little black nightie. I'm not surprised she got laid last night because she was begging for it. I'm surprised she was raped, though. Because I wouldn't have thought rape was necessary."

"She fought," Kellaway said stolidly. "She fought like a wild-cat. She was dead, or half dead, when he did it. That much we know."

I closed my eyes. I wanted to think of her alive, writhing in my arms, little moans in her throat, not fighting off a brutal ravager.

He said, "You heard nothing? Nothing at all?"

"I was working. I had music playing. Loud enough to blanket anything short of a Fireman's Ball."

"You left the door how?"

"After she passed out and after Alma Ward had left, I closed it. I heard the bolt snick shut."

"You didn't try it to see if the lock was set?"

"I had no reason to. I took it for granted."

Kellaway looked down at his desk. He picked up a .45 shell and twirled it. "By the time we got there the lock wasn't set. All anyone had to do was turn the knob and push. Too bad you didn't check when you went out."

"Don't hold it against me."

He snorted. "If the lock wasn't set when you left anyone could have gone in—any prowler in town. If it was locked then either she opened the door for him or he had a key. Knowing even that much would be helpful."

"Prints?"

"Plenty of yours, Stevie boy. Needless to say."

"Oh, hell, say it. I've got skin thicker than a battleship."

"You mentioned a man's picture."

"Yeah. In a leather frame. Senator Tom Quinby. You find his prints?"

His eyes lifted, then looked down again. "Maybe. We'll call that police business for now."

"I see," I said slowly. "Don't think I can't smell a cover-up in the making."

The hand nearest me balled into a fist the size of a maul. His voice was harder than granite. "You know better than that."

"I know better than that where you're concerned. But the D.C. Police Department isn't gilded with gold leaf. The fact that it's run by Congress doesn't make it less political than Kansas City—it makes it a hell of a lot more so. Now slack off and talk sense. Tom Quinby's revolting old face was in that picture frame. Peachy slipped up and mentioned his name to me. She realized what she'd done and got scared, asked me to forget it. The fact that the picture was gone when I found the body means something, and you know it."

"Or nothing," he said carelessly.

"Depending on whether you're looking for the killer."

His jaw jutted out, showing a lot of white teeth. "You know damn well we are. You also know neither I—or anyone else on the force—is going to drag a U.S. Senator down here and brace him as a murder suspect."

"You don't have to do it cold. You can find out who paid Peachy Bolac's rent. There'll be checks, a lease. Hell, it's a routine investigation. As if you didn't know."

"We'll get to all that," he said heavily. "In the meantime what about Alma Ward?"

"I gave you everything that happened. The rest's up to you." I blew smoke toward the spittoon. "Or does her background have you all impressed and nervous?"

"Sure," he said nastily. "Lofty dames in tailored suits always give me the worries. You figure Alma raped her?"

"Not unless she's some new breed of dyke. And God knows, Georgetown breeds all kinds."

"Very funny," Kellaway grunted. "You and old Doc Kinsey."

I said, "I'm your witness that Quinby's picture was there. I'll make a deposition to that effect."

"When you're asked," Kellaway said steadily. "Since you brought it up, why would a man like Senator Quinby rape and kill a girl he was keeping?"

"You'll never know unless you investigate."

He let that one float with the breeze. "Assuming at his age tail meant anything to him, Quinby was getting his share from the girl. And I can't see him killing her out of jealousy."

"I can," I said. "She was scared of him. Not terrified, but scared. If she was the easy flop she looked she might have tried his patience once too often. He killed her that way to make it look like a prowler did it—knowing the police would reason the way you have."

He considered it for a while. Finally his teeth made a sucking sound and he said, "Don't overwork that agile mind just for me. Why not dust off and get back to your neglected profession?"

"Great," I said testily. "Another hugely successful encounter with the Law. Quinby may be too big for you but to me he's just another Throttlebottom. So if you find me poking around the outfield don't throw the outraged act. You had your chance to handle it alone."

He shot me a lidded glance as I stood up. "Simmer down, Steve. We're still working the same side of the street."

"Without telepathy it's hard to tell." I flipped my butt into the spittoon and went out.

A reasonably well lighted hall paved with light marble. Down wide stone steps into a blazing July sun. Only eleven o'clock and you could broil whale steaks on the pavement. I rescued my Olds from the meter and drove over Pennsylvania and up Thirteenth to the parking garage.

As I tramped toward the Washington Building I wondered how many times Kellaway and I had played the same scene. Me needling him and Kellaway fending me off with his cloak of officialdom. We'd been together on a good many cases since the big emerald called the Madagascar Green, and he'd risen a long way from Homicide Lieutenant. But the hostility of the professional for the amateur was still there. Between cases we stayed friends. Hell, how could you stay mad at a cop who raised dwarf Japanese trees?

My hand closed around the card in my pocket and I grinned. I had held out on Kellaway. If he had agreed to take off after Quinby I would have come clean about Peachy's other caller, Jay Redpath. But since Kellaway had gotten snooty about his suspects I would handle the tanned young man myself. In my own way. If there was anything there Kellaway would get it in time. If not, Redpath would have been spared the police blotter. And to a Congressional investigator that would mean a lot.

Riding the elevator up to my office, I cudgeled my brain to recall how and where I had seen Jay Redpath before. It could have been at night school when I was getting my law degree. Just possibly there. But he was a few years younger than I and I had the idea that if he was a lawyer he would have picked up his degree the daytime way. Or maybe I had seen him when I was taking accountancy. Or he could have worked at Treasury in my time, or been in the CID in Korea. There were a lot of possibilities. In any case we would have a chat before many days had passed.

Mrs. Bross was fussing with the electric typewriter when I opened the office door. A carbon ribbon had broken and she looked desperate. Annually, before she took her Old Point Comfort vacation, she grew nervous and next to useless. I wondered how well she kept herself under control, sitting at the bar waiting to be picked up by the Quantico Marine Officers she idolized.

"Call the service shop," I told her breezily. "That's what the service contract's for."

Hastily she arranged her damp hair and riffled through the desk memo pad. "There's been a call for you. At ten o'clock."

"Not another pizzeria," I said wearily. "We've taken absolutely the last spaghetti account. My figure won't take any more free canelonis."

She followed me into the office. I pulled off my coat, hung it up and loosened my tie.

"It's nothing Italian at all," she said primly. "Mr. Bentley, I don't know *how* you do it, but the most *important* people seem to become our clients."

"Oh, rats," I said amiably. "Who called?"

"Mrs. Ward," she said happily. "Mrs. Jeanette Ward. *The* Mrs. Ward. The publisher. Oh, you know, Mr. Bentley."

"I certainly do. You probably think the old gorgon's dismissed her entire staff of lawyers and tax experts and wants me to solve all the problems of her publishing empire. Well, I know better."

"The message was she wants you to call on her today. As soon as you came in."

"She does, does she? Well, call back and see if she can wait half an hour. It'll take me that long to sign checks for all the bills I seem to see littering my desk."

"Yes, sir," she said a little breathlessly, trapped in vicarious excitement.

When the door closed I read the morning mail, signed a few checks, endorsed one from an electronics manufacturer I had kept out of jail and who had expressed his undying appreciation by ignoring my bill for seventeen months. Filling a pipe, I tamped it down and lighted it. Leaning back in my chair, I stared up at the ceiling.

Mrs. Jeanette Ward, widow of Thurston Ward. Dowager head of the Ward publishing enterprises and dam of Alma Ward whom I recalled meeting casually yesterday evening. Of the old lady a disgruntled employee once had said that she was every inch a man—and a tough old turkey at that. I had seen the family manse in Georgetown for years—what you could see of it through tall iron fencing and boxwood hedge—and been properly impressed by the Ward wealth and station. Now I was being summoned by royal command.

My drip-dry suit seemed a little baggy for the suave role I ought to be playing but I wasn't letting it fret me. I had all too clear an idea of what had caused her sudden interest in me and what the outcome would be.

Prying myself out of the chair, I strolled over to the window and stared across the street at the long gray Treasury building. Albert Gallatin stood on his front yard pedestal looking as austere and unconcerned as a wax owl. No pigeons adorned his classic brow, just traces of same. Beyond, I could see shuffling lines of tourists filing into the White House grounds for a rubberneck tour of The Mansh. Like most Washingtonians I had never been inside. Almost the only national monument I had visited was Ford's Theater, and that because of a minx who advertised herself as an authority on Lincolnia. Later discussion with her revealed that she had read one Lincoln poem by Sandburg and a novelized account of Booth's flight. Outside her intellectual qualifications she had been memorable because of her insistence on making love with all lights on and the mirrors artfully arranged. The last I heard of her she was married to a foreman in the Bethlehem Steel shipyard at Sparrows Point, Maryland. Suzie or Elaine or something like that.

Tapping the dottle from my pipe, I pocketed it, tightened my tie and slid into my coat. The night hadn't provided me a surplus of sleep and Mrs. Jeanette Ward would have to overlook the cranberry eyes. I was in that kind of shape.

Mrs. Bross looked up at me and said, "The service man will come as soon as he can after lunch. And Mrs. Ward's secretary said Mrs. Ward will be waiting for you. Good luck, Mr. Bentley."

"Relax," I said. "It's not all that important."

I rode the elevator down to a sweltering street, flagged a cab and settled back against the cushions. We cut over Pennsylvania, drifted around Washington Circle and up 29th to Q Street. West on Q to 31st and up the hill to the lair of the Wards.

I paid the cabbie, got out and straightened my lapels. Above me the high arching branches of elms and locust trees all but hid the sky. The street was shadowed and drowsy in the remote stillness peculiar to Georgetown. Next to Sunset Boulevard, the most coveted real estate in the nation. Once the abode of periwigged Federalists, then slaves, and reclaimed in the past twenty-five years until an address there was a mark of status, a city within a city and the best-policed square mile in the Capital.

The house had been built after the Civil War, high up on Oak Hill, away from freedmen and the mercantile class. It had nothing in common with Georgetown's normally Georgian Colonial red brick and basket arches. It had been clapboard once, the clapboards now surfaced with gray stucco and ornamented by gingerbread scrollwork high under the eaves. A huge three-story house, its slanting entrance walk lined with elms four feet thick. The garden animal statuary was cast iron painted charcoal black. The garden seats were the same and they looked as if nobody had sat in them since the victory at San Juan Hill. Probably nobody had. A sunless house with black louvered shutters and square porch pillars, also black. A well-tended house, but forbidding. Like the dowager who waited inside.

The walk was river-bed slate, polished smooth by the shoe leather of a hundred years. Moss struggled between the cracks. I wondered if moss grew inside the house as well. Or perhaps only mushrooms.

The door was thick with annual layers of black paint and the elms admitted barely enough light to show a button countersunk in the door frame. I pushed it and waited.

Somewhere in the far distance of the house a bell must have sounded because in less than a minute the door opened and a dusky face peered out. Above it a white starched cap. Below it a black maid's outfit with starched white cuffs and a starched bow belt.

"Yes?"

"Mrs. Ward sent for me. My name is Bentley."

"Yes, sir. Please come in."

I stepped up and the maid closed the door behind me.

The dark hallway trailed into an obscure distance. On the right, a walnut staircase covered with a dark runner that looked as if it had been installed yesterday morning. To the left, sliding panel doors. The maid parted them and I went through.

I had once seen another house in Georgetown like it—the old Falconer place on R Street. The same plush-covered furniture from a bygone era, the same antimacassars and corner whatnots.

The same crystal chandelier glinting feebly in light that filtered from the far side of the dark room. Crossing the room, I saw a glassed-in conservatory stocked with potted plants, some taller than my head. The light made me blink and I paused at the doorway to orient myself. The air was moist and warm, heavy with the scent of peat and vegetation, and pungent with chemical fertilizer.

I had to face right to see her. She was seated in a throne-sized chair at the far end, one foot on a plush footstool, her right hand resting on a gold-handled ebony walking stick. Whatever she was wearing had come out of *Godey's Ladies' Book*. Billows of azure silk trimmed with lace and not a few ruffles. The dress fitted her throat closely, eliminating the need for a velvet choker. Instead, I saw a strand of sparkling stones that could have been emerald-cut diamonds and probably were.

Her hair was white and piled untidily above her head. Her face was the face of a willful elderly lady. Piercing eyes, invisible eyebrows and a nose with a strong bend. Her lips were thin and colorless. Lifting a pince-nez, she stared at me for a moment, then rapped her stick sharply on the stone floor.

"Well," she snapped, "it took you long enough to get here."

CHAPTER FOUR

"I reached the office late, Mrs. Ward. I came as soon as I reasonably could after getting your message."

"You a late sleeper, young man?"

"When the neighbors let me."

She harrumphed, rapped the cane on the floor again and beckoned me closer. Dropping the pince-nez in her lap, she squinted up at me. In a harsh voice she said, "Evidently the neighbors indulged you today."

"Yeah. One neighbor died last night—in a manner of speaking. Except for a few idle hours I've been with the police since then."

That rocked her back against the high crown of her chair. The cane end rattled against the floor and she barked, "What did the police want with you?"

I glanced at a straight-backed chair and eased myself into it. She hadn't invited me, but she didn't object. Crossing my legs, I said, "Suppose we bypass that for the moment and get to why you summoned me here. Believe it or not, Mrs. Ward, I have a business that's fairly demanding."

Her lips tightened, she stared at me even more piercingly and leaned forward. "I want you to work for me."

I said nothing.

She rasped, "You're a Certified Public Accountant. Well, I could use one. Oh, I have a flock of them, but they're vultures, plucking the money from my newspapers. I want some fresh blood."

"To drink?"

She blinked and her mouth opened and shut. Her face turned pink. One foot shoved the footstool aside and she snapped, "Give me a cigarette."

I flushed one for her and lighted it. I did the same for myself. She lifted her head, inhaled deeply and blew smoke at the leaves of a rubber plant. She had a serviceable pair of lungs. I waited for the plant to crumple. Finally she said, "At least you have a mind of your own. I'm sick of flatterers and sycophants. Well, what about it?"

"What's your offer?"

"Double your last year's income."

I shook my head. "As a bachelor that would only put me in a higher tax bracket. Beside I like working for myself. I put in a lot of long years trying to become independent. I like it that way."

Her eyes narrowed. "You don't like money?"

"I like it well enough. There happen to be other things in life I like equally well. Now suppose we talk about the real reason I'm here, Mrs. Ward. Evidently your daughter told you I saw her in Miss Bolac's apartment yesterday night. Probably nobody else did. If the Ward clan is anything it's close-mouthed and wary about personal publicity. I think you panicked and decided the best way to keep me from talking was to hire me, buy me off." I stood up, dropped ash on a potted plant and said, "It was never a good idea but in any case it's useless now."

"Useless?"

"Quite useless. As any co-operative citizen would I gave the police an account of what went on at Miss Bolac's apartment last evening. Including your daughter's visit. Do you use a pipe, Mrs. Ward?"

Her eyes glinted suspiciously. "Why?"

"I was going to suggest you put that in your pipe and smoke it."

"Sit down, young man," she raged. "Nobody's talked to me like that in thirty years!"

I stayed on my feet. "That's too long to have your own way. We could have settled all this by telephone, but I doubt if you've learned the dial system. Anyway, I'm not letting myself be hired and I've told the police Alma came to Peachy Bolac's apartment last night. On business—nature unknown. That seems to be about all. Except that I don't really mind having come here. I've often wondered what this place would be like. I wondered, too, what you were like. Not that it means anything but from our remote distance I've always half admired you. I'd admire anyone of your sex and years who could take over and run as tough a man's job as old Thurston left you. Now I know how you did it."

"You do?" Her voice had softened. "Perhaps you'll tell me."

"By bullying. By scaring everyone who came in contact with you. It's that simple. The power of money."

She blinked again and her face seemed to relax. "Please sit down, Mr. Bentley. I think we ought to talk a little more."

I sat down and she leaned forward. The edge had left her voice and she said, "Very well, I wanted to buy you off. I failed and I'm not accustomed to failure. Around here I'm used to doing things pretty much my own way."

I nodded, set the gasper between my lips and waited.

She said, "We'll forget the offer I made you. It was a mistake on my part, and as you pointed out, too late in any case. I wanted to keep Alma out of the papers. Her TV program is important to her—and to me—and I rather think you can imagine how sleazy publicity could damage it." She shifted the cane to her other hand and cleared her throat. I could feel sweat soaking into my shirt collar. She went on: "I have no idea how well you knew the late Loris Bolac, but for your information, she was the kept woman of a United States Senator."

"Tom Quinby."

"Quite right. Senator Quinby's wife has been in a madhouse for the past nine years. Her background was not such that she could cope with the requirements of Washington social life and she sought refuge from her inadequacies in insanity. It's not uncommon. So the Senator was entitled, I suppose, to conduct himself as he saw fit." She lifted a fragile, veined hand. "In itself that is not important. Miss Bolac would have been useful only if she had been able to provide my daughter with certain evidence which could have exposed Senator Quinby."

"As what?"

"As a henchman of Larry Zellerhaus." Her eyebrows lifted. "The name is not unfamiliar?"

"I've heard of him. The influence-peddler. The big fixer."

"Posing as a lobbyist. Both Alma and I have reason to believe that Zellerhaus paid Quinby substantial sums for doing his special dirty work. That is what we hoped to prove."

"What kind of evidence did Miss Bolac have?"

"Perhaps none. On the other hand she may have known a good deal that could have led to evidence sufficiently tangible to discredit both Quinby and Zellerhaus. As you may know, a senator's sources of income are supposed to be a matter of public record. That can be avoided of course by having bribes paid to close relatives, by having anonymous bank accounts and safe-deposit boxes. It is the existence and nature of those that we hoped to disclose." She laid her cane beside her knee and opened her hands. "So you see there is nothing discreditable in what Alma was trying to do."

"It depends on how you look at it. Some people might think that suborning a man's mistress against his interests verged on the discreditable."

"Against the public good?"

"Who's to say?" I got up, shook out my trousers and ran a finger inside my collar. "Anyway, why tell me? If Quinby's a wrong-doer it will come to light in time."

She snorted. "I can't believe you're that innocent. If you are I should congratulate you. Or pity you."

"It's turned out to be a day filled with homilies, Mrs. Ward. Suppose we overlook my unworldliness long enough for an easy question."

"Very well."

"Does the name Redpath mean anything to you? Jay Redpath?"

"Of course it does."

"In what connection?"

Something moved behind her eyes. It could have been hate or sudden compassion. "Jay Redpath is my son-in-law. Alma's husband."

It stiffened me. His card was in my hand, hidden in my pocket. "That clears it up nicely," I lied and let the card drop free.

"I don't know why it should clear up anything at all. Is Jay in trouble?"

"None that I know of."

I thought I heard a faint sigh of relief. Pulling my hand from my pocket, I said, "He's an attorney, isn't he?"

"Yes. He never had a successful practice. At present I believe he is connected with some legislative committee or other."

"But you wouldn't know?"

She gathered herself erect and plucked at the cane handle. "Jay and my daughter have been separated for nearly two years, Mr. Bentley. If that's any business of yours."

"None at all."

"It happens to have been a fairly amicable separation—in the modern sense. Alma, needless to say, could have maintained them both very comfortably, but Jay insisted on being the bread-winner. It didn't work out."

"It seldom does," I said. "If the man's got any spine."

Her eyes flashed at that. "Is there anything else, Mr. Bentley?"

"Nothing, ma'am. I take it I'm free to leave?"

"Entirely. If such is required I appreciate your having come. And I don't for one moment believe that Jay isn't somehow involved in all this. Isn't he?"

"Let's hope not," I said, turned, and strode down the long lane between the towering green plants.

The air in the living room was cooler. A lot cooler. It was also free of the chemicals that had made my eyes smart. Maybe she got something out of sitting there inhaling them. Maybe I would too when I reached her age. If I managed it.

The maid was standing in the hall. She opened the door with the unobtrusive grace of a well-trained servant and bade me good-by. Then I was on the porch, filling my lungs with expensive Georgetown air.

In the driveway stood a car. A maroon Riley with shiny chrome trimmings. It wasn't as large as a Rolls but it wasn't much smaller, either. The door opened and a woman got out. The door closed with a well-machined sound and the woman crossed toward the walk.

She was wearing dark teardrop glasses and a white poplin dress. As she walked I could see the motion of a very full bosom. Her tanned legs were long, tapering into thin ankles. If any nylon covered them it was invisible. I waited for her at the bottom of the steps. When she looked up she uttered a little cry and lifted her handbag. I said, "Good day, Mrs. Redpath."

"Oh," she said uncertainly. "Good morning."

I let her come toward me. When she was a yard away I glanced back at the house and said, "Whose idea was it? Yours or the old gorgon's?"

Her face tightened. "I don't believe I understand, Mr. Bentley."

"Go on with you. The plan to buy me off and shut my mouth forever. I wasn't particularly tempted and I wasn't outraged. Just mildly amused."

She humphed and started to brush past but I caught her wrist. "The police know you were there," I said roughly.

She shook my hand away and massaged her wrist. Her cheeks were drained of color. "You were there too," she said hostilely.

"There were several people on the scene last night, Mrs. Redpath. Apart from ourselves there was the murderer. Let's not ever forget him."

She bit her lower lip. Glancing down she said, "Do the police—"

"The police are hard at work, if that's your question. I have another: what did your husband want with Peachy Bolac? The same as you wanted? Or was the motive less noble?"

Even through her tinted lenses I could see the roundness of her eyes. Throatily she said, "I haven't the least idea."

"And you could care less." I shrugged. "Well, one confidence begets another. If it will improve your day I wouldn't worry about police publicity. Kellaway wouldn't be where he is if he didn't know when to talk and when to keep his mouth shut. As if you didn't know."

Her mouth opened, she breathed deeply and the remarkable bosom undulated. Why the hell would a woman with a body like that want to be anything other than just a woman? She said, "Please let me pass."

I nodded thoughtfully. "Fate or circumstance seems to have thrown us together, Mrs. Redpath. I barely knew Loris Bolac but I'd like to see her killer caught and roasted. Your interest in her may have ended with her death but mine began there. I'm a bachelor and I live alone. From time to time I do what I can for the police—unofficially of course—and any thoughts you might have regarding Peachy's fate would be more than welcome."

Her handbag lowered slowly. She glanced down, then up. She seemed to be considering my suggestion. Abruptly her chin lifted and she said, "Very well. I don't know why, but I have a vague feeling I can trust you. Perhaps I could help you. And you might be useful to me."

Her tongue flicked across her upper lip in a quick serpentine movement. In that moment she was preening herself unguardedly, utterly redolent of sex. "If you care to talk to me tonight, I have a house on Volta Place. Say about seven-thirty."

"I'll be there."

Then the mask snapped on again and she moved past me, her heels making soft leathery sounds on the smooth slate. Turning I watched her go up the stairs and enter the house. The big black door closed and I was alone.

As I walked toward the street a spotted flicker swooped down from an elm and perched on the antler of an iron stag. It squawked a few times, flapped its wings and soared away. Beyond the boxwood barrier the street was silent. Nothing had changed. Nothing except that my palms were slippery. The day was improving hour by hour. I wondered what evening on Volta Place would bring.

I had to walk over to Wisconsin to look for a cab. Standing on the corner, I surveyed Nance Alley baking in the noonday sun. From where I stood I could count three antique stores, two interior decoration shops, a laundry, a faggoty art gallery, two restaurants and a grocery that sold only imported victuals. Plus a package store, a tearoom run by an admiral's widow, a laundromat and a drugstore notorious for what it provided the teen-age trade. A cab skidded to a stop beside the curb but I waved it away and walked into the drugstore. The card in my pocket gave me the number I wanted. I dialed it and asked for Mr. Redpath.

The secretary demanded my name so I supplied her with it and after a whispered discussion I heard Redpath's voice inquiring what I wanted.

I said, "We had a chat last evening when you were ringing Peachy's bell. If you wondered why the police haven't been around to talk to you it's because I lifted your card from the door, sparing you that inconvenience."

"Say," he said in a relieved voice, "I certainly appreciate you doing that."

"That's as it should be. I'd like to see you in my office as soon after lunch as convenient. About two."

Thoughtful silence. Finally, "I have appointments most of the afternoon, Mr. Bentley. Couldn't we make it tomorrow?"

"We could, but I've a busy day. I recommend you make it at two, Mr. Redpath. Anything you might have planned seems trivial beside the card you left in Peachy's door and the fact that the police are keenly interested in grilling suspects."

"All right," he said shortly. "I'll come."

"Washington Building," I told him and hung up.

As I pushed out of the booth I could see a girl about sixteen leaning against the paperbook rack, leafing through the latest lust sensation. She wore sneakers, white wool socks, a well-filled blouse and blue shorts so tight she deserved to be dragged off and serviced. Then I remembered how Peachy had looked leaning against her doorway and I turned cold inside.

A cab took me to The Embers where I had a light dietary lunch: double mutton chop, baked Idaho, salad from a bowl big enough to wade in, and two frosty bottles of Heineken's lager. After that I waddled out to the street and cabbed back to the office.

CHAPTER FIVE

Redpath was there at two, all right. Not a minute before and not a minute after. In a light cord suit, Madras bow tie and thirty-dollar cordovans. His face was flushed, as though he had walked too fast or inhaled a couple of Gibsons too many along with the noonday prime ribs.

Mrs. Bross closed the door behind him and he found himself a chair. Crossing his legs, he stared at me defiantly. "Before you say anything I ought to warn you that I am an attorney. And my position with the Joint Congressional Committee gives me certain powers and immunities."

"Why the prologue?"

He flushed. "You may be thinking of trying to blackmail me."

I snapped the pencil in my hand and pushed back from my desk. "Once more, Mr. Redpath," I said levelly.

His face paled. "Why, I—"

"I don't like the word blackmail, and I get irritable when it's applied to me, however unwittingly. You married a wealthy woman, Mr. Redpath, but you couldn't hold the pace by your own means. So you hooked a job with the government, the last refuge of the inept and incompetent. Don't try to impress me with what you can push around. It doesn't happen to be a hell of a lot."

He said nothing. His hands fussed with the seam of his coat. I selected a pipe from the rack, filled it and got it going. Leaning back in my chair, I said, "Your wife called on Peachy last evening not long before you got there. Peachy was passed out and of no value to anyone. Later, when you asked about Peachy I clammed up, not knowing anything about you. I worked in my apartment last night with the hi-fi going. When I went to bed I couldn't sleep, so about three o'clock I went out for a stroll. As I passed Peachy's door it was open. I had a funny feeling about it—premonition, perhaps—and so I went inside. I found the body."

He wiped his forehead with the side of his hand. "Did Alma get to talk with her?"

"No. And especially not about Senator Quinby. It's a reasonable assumption that both of you were interested in Peachy for the same shabby reason. Or maybe you were laying her as well."

White spots appeared under his eyes. "I don't have to answer that."

"Hell," I said, "nobody's investigating your morals. And Peachy had two of the roundest heels in town, so don't chalk her up as a triumph in seduction. Now, from what I know so far I judge that you and Alma had conflicting interests in Peachy and the Senator. At least there's no evidence you were co-operating."

"Alma wanted to break the case on her TV program," he said bitterly. "She'd do anything for a Pulitzer Prize—that's what she lives and dreams. The Committee isn't interested in sensationalism and headlines. My job is to get evidence of Senator Quinby's alleged misconduct, and nail him down. Along with Larry Zellerhaus—if he's been bribing Quinby."

"You have substantial reason to believe that?"

He looked uncomfortable. "That's privileged information."

I let it drift by. "What about Zellerhaus?"

He brightened. "He's a front for Maury Renzo—the Baltimore racketeer."

"So people say. It might be a lot harder to prove. I've had a couple of waltzes with Maury Renzo and foxes could take lessons from him. To spare you a little time I might mention that Renzo doesn't bank in this country. He uses cash in his operations—truck-loads of it. When he needs to make a transfer he or one of his lieutenants makes a quiet trip to Geneva or Bern and

brings back the boodle in bearer checks. How Zellerhaus oper-
ates I don't know, but as a registered lobbyist he has to file annual
statements of income and disbursements."

"Anybody knows that," he said shortly and fingered the end
of his tie.

"How did Alma find out about Peachy and the Senator?"

"I'm not answering that."

"Hell, I can ask her. If it was a government secret once, Alma's
learning it cancels the classification. You guys are all the same.
You won't bite a sardine sandwich without taking an oath."

He sat forward. "I didn't come here to have you abuse me."

"Relax," I told him. "This is a tough town. All the pretty public
buildings don't mean a thing. There're more crimes of violence,
more rape, more incest and felony per capita than any other city
in the country. And some of the District fleshpots would embar-
rass a Panama pimp. In short, anybody doing any investigating
around here had better leave the doeskin gloves in his bureau
and get familiar with brass knuckles. The reason for all this, I
might add, is that our lofty Congress governs the District. If we
had an elected Mayor and a Board of Supervisors responsible to
the voters things might change. But the District resident has less
recourse than a lifer on Devil's Island."

He glanced down at his watch. "Is there anything else,
Mr. Bentley?"

"I guess not," I said wearily. "For the present your secret's
safe with me."

He stood up. "I guess you mean well," he said haltingly.
"Maybe I'm not used to such complete frankness."

"It's anything but that." I stood up. "Tell me, does Quinby
know he's under investigation?"

"I certainly hope not."

"I'll try to remember."

He turned, crossed to the door and went out. Sighing I
relighted my pipe. Mrs. Bross came in, half looking over her

shoulder. "Such a nice-looking young man, Mr. Bentley. So gentlemanly."

"That may be his entire trouble." I sat down and let her slide things in front of me to sign. Then she went away. Friday night she would be riding the cruise boat down to Old Point Comfort and two weeks of artificial paradise. In a way I would be glad to see her go. The summer had been paralyzingly hot, with more than its share of troubles. I had been getting increasingly short with her and a vacation from each other would do us both good. A bachelor and a grass-widow spinster made an unlikely combination. But she was a no-nonsense assistant, and she lent the office an air of serious purpose that clients liked. So she stayed on. With her powers of endurance she would probably bury me.

I got up and adjusted the air-conditioner for cooler air. No client was due until four o'clock and I was at reasonably loose ends. Once the fiscal year business ends, summer is the slack season in taxes and I had determined more than once to devote an August to sailing my ketch down the Inland Waterway perhaps as far as Florida. But something had always come up. Once it had been Maury Renzo.

Maury Renzo. I visualized his tortured, intelligent face, prey to ulcers like any other high-powered executive. I remembered his country-gentleman manners, his carefully tailored clothes and I thought of two hawk-faced gunmen who were no longer among the living. I was responsible for that and he knew it. Some day it would be just the two of us, a soundproof room, two guns and winner take all.

Thinking about it had coated my forehead with sweat. I brushed it off, shook myself back to the present and Larry Zellerhaus.

He was a lobbyist who spent plenty of green, lived like a millionaire and traveled first class wherever he went. His estate was over the line in Fairfax County not far from Little Falls. Not more than forty acres of lush bluegrass breeding Black Angus and pedigreed show horses. He would be about right for Maury Renzo. Their tastes had a lot in common. And Senator Tom Quinby would be about right for Larry Zellerhaus. A Senatorial salary is something less than a uranium lode and nine years of sanitarium bills for a schizoid wife would subtract quite a lot of it. Plus campaign expenses and the high cost of living in Washington, plus maintaining little Angel Eyes. I could understand how money from Zellerhaus would come in handy to Old Bubblenose. The trick was to prove it. The gentlemanly Mr. Redpath would need more than just a little luck.

At four my client arrived, deposited his problems with me, and left on a lighthearted flight to Saratoga Springs for the harness meet. At five o'clock Mrs. Bross called through the intercom to announce a Mr. Lester Nagle.

He was a tall man in undertaker's black with matching hair, a wispy mustache and a violet tie. Dropping a card on my desk he moved away and settled himself primly in a chair. The card bore his name and a legend describing himself as Administrative Assistant to Senator Quinby. I looked up from it and decided that I did not like Mr. Nagle from the tips of his pointed and polished black shoes to the top of his wavy black hair. His entrance had brought with it the cloying scent of barbershop bay rum. He was too neat, too smug and I sensed something of the nance about him.

"Yes, Mr. Nagle. What can I do for you?"

His hands unfolded and he sat forward slightly. His voice was the flat, slightly arrogant voice of the career bureaucrat. "Perhaps a great deal."

"Say on."

He cleared his throat delicately. "You live in an apartment next to that occupied by the unfortunate Miss Bolac."

"I do."

He lifted his hand to his mouth, covered it and coughed slightly. Against a face as white as cold tallow his lips were unusually pink. "Her demise poses a problem for Senator Quinby." His eyes darted at me hopefully but I gave him no help. His hand fluttered and he shifted his shoulders uneasily. "You were a friend of Miss Bolac's, perhaps?"

"Perhaps."

Fingers drummed against his kneecap. "I see. A close friend, perhaps?"

"Perhaps."

He leaned forward. "Did she ever say anything about Senator Quinby?"

"She did."

A shadow crossed his face. In the depths of his dark eyes something moved. He swallowed and said, "You realize in what a difficult position her death places the Senator?"

"Why not tell me."

He smiled unhappily. The fingers drummed more rapidly. I had the feeling he was going to start spinning like a top. Maybe right out of the door. I hoped the bay rum would go with him.

His voice rose a minor third. "Publicity connecting Miss Bolac and the Senator would be most unfortunate."

"It's one of the things to be considered in setting up a love nest."

Nagle blinked. "Please, Mr. Bentley, I hope you're not going to be difficult."

"I've been known to be. Depending on circumstances." I smiled innocently at him.

Warily he said, "The Senator would be most appreciative if you managed to eliminate his name from any conversations you might hold with the police."

"Think of that," I murmured. "Couldn't the Senator say as much himself? Or has grief overwhelmed him?"

"One could say he has been deeply touched by Miss Bolac's unfortunate death."

"It wasn't exactly a death," I snarled. "She was raped and murdered. Her killer's at large. It happened while I was home next door. It happened not many hours after Miss Bolac and I had been enjoying a neighborly drink. It sticks in my guts that it happened at all. Unfortunate—you're damn right it was unfortunate. And the man who should be mourning her doesn't come here himself to ask a reasonable courtesy of me—instead he sends you, a pimp in reverse. From that I get the idea he's busier worrying about next election than avenging Peachy's death. You don't draw a picture of much of a man for me, Mr. Nagle. Senator Quinby may be hell on wheels to you, but to me he's a pawing old lecher squirming in the clutches of conscience. I say the hell with him. If word gets around about him and Peachy it's still short of his due. If you need a message to take back to the Senator that's the best I can manage on short notice."

His face purpled. Fumbling with his violet tie, he jumped to his feet and waved a long finger at me. "You'll regret this, Bentley!" he nearly screamed. "The Senator's got influence in a lot of places!"

"Around the outhouse crowd. And tuck away that finger before I snap it off. If I had my way the Senator would be down at Headquarters sweating it out under a hot bulb. And he may be yet. Add that to the foregoing. Now scat!"

Nagle pivoted and pounced at the door. Wrenching it open, he scuttled out. The stench of bay rum was stronger than ever.

I yanked open a window and let a wave of hot air slide into the office. If it carried coal dust and oil fumes it smelled better than Nagle's perfume. Quinby's piney woods constituents would love that.

Mrs. Bross was standing at the door, mumbling something.

"Speak up," I yelled.

"Please—please, Mr. Bentley." She fidgeted, straightened a bind in her dress and said, "I never should have announced him."

"Hell, he's got winning ways. A perfect lady." I shook my head disgustedly. The burr of the phone cut the atmosphere like a buzz saw.

Picking it up I heard Kellaway's voice. Mrs. Bross edged back through the door. Kellaway was purring, "Thought you might like to know the case is all but sewed up."

"Do tell." I sank into my chair, fished out a cigarette and lighted it. With one hand. My lips were dry.

"Yeah," he said condescendingly. "The building janitor—maybe you know him—Ray Stroud. He's down here now, sweating it out. We figure on a confession by midnight."

"What kind of evidence?"

"Tell me about that picture frame that was supposed to hold Quinby's picture."

"Natural leather," I rasped. "Calf or possibly pigskin. Saddle-stitched with tan thread. Reasonably new. About eight by ten."

A long chuckle. "If I didn't have it here in front of me I could draw the picture myself."

"You found it where?"

"Stroud's room. He said he found it in a trash barrel in the alley."

"Why not?"

"Huh?"

"Look, I'm not trying to dilute the sweet savor of triumph, but I've known Ray better than four years and if he's the killer I'm Secretary of State. I don't doubt you'll get a confession out of him; hell, by midnight you could have him swearing he swiped the Washington Monument."

Kellaway's voice was dry. "Fortunately I don't have to convince you. A jury's more reasonable."

"On convincing evidence. What you've got is only circumstantial and you know it. A sharp jawsmith will dispose of it before the jury's warmed its chairs."

"Like hell."

"You're leading from weakness," I snapped. "Arraign him and they'll laugh you out of court. What was in the frame?"

"Nothing," he said slowly. "Not a damn thing."

"Of course not. The killer ripped out the picture and tossed the frame away. The killer, I said, not Ray Stroud. Admit it, you don't like this any better than I do. But there's an advantage to be gained."

"Yeah?" The jeer was gone from his voice.

"Yeah. Put out word you've jailed a suspect. The killer will find out and relax, maybe even do something foolish. Ray will co-operate, but for Christ's sake tell him he's not under active suspicion."

Kellaway let out a long sigh. "You and your hunches. You should play the races."

"Think it over," I said soothingly. "Do the smart thing. By the way, an emissary from Senator Quinby just left here."

"No kidding. What'd he want?"

"What you'd expect. The Senator would take it very favorably if I wouldn't mention his connection with Peachy Bolac."

"You don't say. And your reply?"

"If I told you they'd cancel my phone service."

"I'll be damned," he said thoughtfully. "I guess the Senator's worried."

"He has reason to be. If no one claims the body you might bill him for burial costs. He'll pay."

"That's a thought," Kellaway chuckled. "Suppose I take a chance on Stroud. Anyone go his bond?"

"Me," I said, "and thanks."

He started getting gruff again and I hung up. When I looked around, the reception office light was off, Mrs. Bross had gone home. That made it after five-thirty. Two hours and I had a date with Alma Ward.

I buttoned up the office and drove home.

CHAPTER SIX

Her house was a one and a half story salt-box set back from the walk, not far from the big corner manse where Alexander Graham Bell had lived. It was Bell who had given Volta Place its name.

For a Colonial wooden house it looked solid and well cherished. The white boards had seen spring painting and the green shutters glowed like polished jade. There were two carriage lamps beside the doorway, antique ones with bull's-eye glass, and pegged to the door a painted fire plaque dated 1819.

Air-conditioners hung out of every window, the house would be too old for central conditioning. Elsewhere in the country the house might pass as a bungalow for a small family, not very modern, not very chic, but in Georgetown it was worth a cool seventy grand as it stood. Termites and all. When you got to know Washington you learned that the Nation's affairs were run from houses like this. Your neighbor could be a Cabinet Secretary, the Senate Majority Leader, or an internationally famous opinion-maker. A small inbred colony of the rich and powerful with private lives as walled as their gardens.

The sun had long since vanished but there was plenty of evening light remaining. I took off my hat, wiped the headband and put it back on. Then I rang the bell.

The green door had polished brass trim. It opened inward and I saw a girl in a navy silk blouse with matching lounge slacks. Her ankles were bare and she wore spike-heeled white sandals. Her bracelet was a heavy gold chain festooned with large antique gold coins. The throat of her blouse lay open and her dark hair hung below her shoulders. Mrs. Jay Redpath, otherwise known as Alma Ward. I doffed my hat and entered. As she shut the door she said, "You made quite an impression on my mother."

"She's pretty impressive herself." I laid my hat on a curly maple table, flexed my arms and glanced through the terrace doorway. A fieldstone terrace opened onto a sunken garden that looked as if it had been manicured earlier in the day. The encircling wall was old red brick dripping with ivy and roses. She said, "Let's have our drinks out there before the mosquitoes descend."

"I thought they weren't permitted in Georgetown."

"If we stay long enough you'll see." She led the way outside and there were comfortable cushioned wrought-iron chairs and a Sheffield tray of drinks on a folding iron table. "Maid's night off," Alma said. "Suppose you handle the drinks. Scotch mist for me."

Arranging herself in a russet-leather safari chair she lighted a cigarette and watched me build our drinks. Her slacks were tight enough to have been painted on. She took hers from me and straightened her blouse. I found a chair and sat down.

When I had moistened my tonsils I said, "The police have arrested a man for Peachy's murder."

Her eyebrows lifted. Breathing was suspended.

"No one you know," I said casually. "Unless you know the building janitor, Ray Stroud."

"No," she said in an odd voice. "I never heard of him. Did he confess?"

"Not according to my information. But that's no trick. You start out with a confession and prove the case from there."

"You sound as though you might know something of criminal matters."

"Something."

"As a hobby?"

"Chance, mostly."

She was gazing at me reflectively. "When I learned of Peachy's murder the first person I thought of was you."

"And the second?"

Very slowly she put her cigarette to her lips, inhaled and let smoke trickle from her nostrils. "Obviously you meant something by that!"

"I may have. Then again it might just have been defense reaction to an implied accusation."

Her head inclined slightly. "You'll admit it was a rather sordid little scene I came across. I suppose you'd slept with her."

"Would it make a difference?"

Spots of color appeared on her cheeks. "Why should it?"

I shrugged. "When Peachy moved in I was down in Saint Thomas. An hour before you arrived I'd never seen her."

"Then what makes you so interested in the case?"

"What made your mother—and you—so interested in me?"

Her face turned away. "You went through that with mother."

"So I did. What I didn't take up with her was the fact that not long after you'd flounced off, your husband was pounding Peachy's door. I talked with Jay this afternoon."

"About what?" Her voice picked up a harmonic of urgency.

"We talked some about Peachy. And we talked about Old Scissorbill Quinby, Peachy's alleged protector."

"Alleged, nothing. He was keeping her."

"You can't prove that."

"I'm not sure I want to." She held out her glass. "Sweeten this, will you?"

I crawled out of my chair and obliged. Then I did the same for myself. There was a rock pool at the end of the garden and beyond a couple of graceful arches. At first I thought they opened onto more garden but then I saw that they were inset with mirrors. Nodding at them, I said, "Quaint."

"Oh, that. They fool nearly everybody the first time."

"Like you," I said, handing her the refill.

Her lips took an angry set. "What, exactly, do you mean by that?"

Sitting back in my chair, I grinned at her. "The first time we talked I had you figured for a high-priced lady lawyer who put career above the better things in life. I also figured you as a stuffed shirt with all the animation of a robot." I lifted my glass and peered at her across the rim. "The second time we met my ideas began to change. And now..." I sipped my drink, dabbed my mouth with a handkerchief and smiled winningly.

"Well?" She was sitting forward, her knuckles white, her face stony.

I leaned back in my chair and surveyed her comfortably. "Do you always do that with your hair when you're home, Alma?"

One hand shot to her lowered tresses. Her head tossed angrily and she husked, "Aren't you getting presumptuous, Mr. Bentley?"

"Steve to my friends," I murmured. "I've also been accused of impertinence. This very day. I ought to apologize and promise to strive for self-betterment, but I'm an old offender. And what else could you expect from the boy friend of that cheap little booster, Peachy Bolac?"

"You said you *weren't* her boy friend." She colored at the last word. I hooked one knee over the other and lighted a cigarette. A light scent of jasmine was beginning to drift across the garden. We could have been in the middle of a forest instead of a city.

Her eyes lowered, she did something to her bracelet and pushed hair back from her forehead. It gave her a wanton look. That and the full dark lips, the haughty eyes. I said, "Why not stop trying to be the man your father was or the martinet your mother is and take life as it comes? Having a nationwide TV program like yours must be richly satisfying, but there are other things in life."

"Such as?" she said defiantly.

I sat forward and rested my elbow on one knee. "Want me to say them?"

That jarred her. Her lips moved and finally she said huskily, "No, don't. I don't want you to."

"I thought not. But I can't help observing it's a tremendous waste of talent."

The light was dim but I could have sworn I saw her blush. Almost tremulously she said, "I'm a married woman, Steve."

"But not working at it. I doubt you ever really worked at it. Hell, you had your TV program. Isn't that what every woman really wants?"

Her hands had clenched the points of her chair. Her eyes flashed as she said, "I'll have to take my mother's place some day—the way she took over from my father. Three newspapers and two radio stations require more managerial talent than the ordinary housewife can muster. I've spent my life preparing to run our business and if I haven't had time for pots and pans and diapers that's the reason." Her eyes narrowed as she settled back slowly. "Something men can't stand is a successful woman executive. You talk about other things in life when all you really mean is sex. That's the sole thing the male can provide. Well, I know what sex is all about and it leaves something to be desired. You deprecate my career when all you really are is envious."

For her it was a long speech. Listening to it and watching her deliver it made it seem even longer. Her breast was heaving and her lips must have gone dry. The tip of her tongue moistened them.

I chuckled and smiled sunnily. "Maybe so. Certainly my career doesn't stand comparison to yours. Now that we've tested our lances let's stack them and talk about Larry Zellerhaus."

That brought her forward in a hurry. "Who told you about him?"

"Your husband. He's interested in Larry Zellerhaus equally with you. And Senator Quinby. A laudable interest. Properly followed, in official channels, it might turn into something memorable."

"It will die in official channels," she said bitterly. "You don't know the Hill as I do. And Jay"—she spread her hands—"Jay couldn't track down an umbrella on a rainy night."

"He seems to be trying."

Her face slanted away. "I'd rather not discuss it."

I laughed shortly. "You want to break it as a news sensation. Some people might find that a trifle short-sighted."

"You among them?"

"And self-serving."

Her hands balled into little fists. "Stop it! Stop it! No one can tell me what's right and what's wrong. I know what I have to do and I'm doing it. No one can stop me!"

"Don't count on that, sugar. With Maury Renzo off in the background this is the Big League. Men with full-scale investigative resources, money and ample motivation have spent long years trying to spread-eagle Maury Renzo. Most of them are retired, broke, out of business or dead. Yet Maury Renzo goes on. If he's been using Senator Quinby through Zellerhaus he'll fight to protect him. Peachy Bolac is dead, raped the police say. That doesn't rule out a hired killer set on her because she became a threat to Zellerhaus and Renzo. You were in touch with her to get at Quinby, so was Jay Redpath. I can imagine the amount of discretion with which Angel Eyes would handle something clandestine like that. Her idea of secrecy would be to blurt the whole thing to five girl friends, any one of whom might have passed the word back to Zellerhaus or Renzo. Or even someone else."

Fear slid across her face. Over her cheekbones the skin was as taut as parchment. I said, "I don't say you're in danger, but someone got to Peachy. I don't think the janitor killed her and I don't think a prowl-thief broke in. Neither one would have had cause to take Quinby's picture. Even though Quinby figures in this I doubt mightily that he's the killer—at his age passion seldom rules. That makes it someone to whom Peachy represented a menace so long as she lived. What kind of evidence was she going to sell you?"

She was drawn into her chair, almost huddled. "A recording," she whispered. "Zellerhaus used to meet Quinby there and give him orders. I found out from Jay."

"His own worst enemy."

Her lips firmed. "I lent her a small recorder, absolutely noiseless. One day before they came in she hid it under the sofa and went out. When she came back they were gone. The recording lasted nearly an hour."

"But she wouldn't give it to you."

"She wanted more money. I went there last night to pay it."

"How much?"

"I gave her a thousand dollars to begin with. Then she wanted five thousand more. I had it with me last night. And the little tramp got drunk!"

"Worse, she got killed."

Her face sobered and she nodded slowly. "You're right. She's dead, poor thing." One hand swept back her hair. She shivered, got up and spilled scotch into her glass. Closing her eyes, she faced around and tossed it off. Then she gasped and opened her eyes. "That shows me the heartless bitch I am. How right you were." She seemed to slump. Unsteadily she made her way back to the chair and sat down. Tonelessly she said, "I planned to invite Quinby to appear on my program, Zellerhaus too. Then when the program was underway I was going to play the recording."

"At least the Pulitzer," I said. "Maybe the Nobel Prize as well."

She looked away. "All gone," she said in a remote voice. "All finished. And it cost the little thing her life."

"Greed did that," I said. "You weren't really responsible. Like most tramps Angel Eyes had the soul of a grifter. She was willing to betray Quinby and she held you up for more dough. For her the combination was fatal."

A long sigh. Finally a muffled voice. "Thanks for putting it that way. In any case I'll never forgive myself." She looked back at me and there was color in her cheeks again. High color. " 'Nother drink?"

"Sure." I got up, added cubes and sauce to her glass and handed it back. I was getting a little lightheaded myself. I poured a thin one and leaned against the trunk of a tree. As she drank she seemed to waver slightly. I was better off. I had the tree behind me.

Darkness was dropping rapidly. I could barely see the glint of the mirrors at the foot of the garden. Somewhere a frog croaked. From the rock pool, probably. It was a night to run shoeless through grass, a night to bathe in moonlight. I glanced down at her and saw that she was gazing up at me. In a quiet voice she said, "I have to admit you're quite a fellow."

"And you're quite a lady."

Her mouth made a motion of distaste. "Whatever that means."

"It means whatever you want it to."

Lifting her glass, she drained it, coughed and handed it to me. Empty. "Want another," she slurred. "How 'bout you?"

"I'm on sort of a diet," I said. "I try to space my drinking with food now and then."

"Food," she said sulkily. "I'm on a diet, too."

"With *that* figure?"

It pleased her. She looked up at me as though I'd just handed her the key to a palace. "Like it?" she asked, lifted her arms and stretched. The blouse must have been reinforced with spun steel. No silk could have withstood that much pressure. I studied her admiringly and said, "I'm crazy about it."

"Then why don't you do something about it?"

With one hand I pulled her to her feet. With the other I drew her against me. A glass crashed against stone but I barely heard it. Her breath filled my mouth, then her tongue. Her arms were strong, her breasts flattened against me. After a while I said, "Was this what you had in mind?"

"For a start." Her thighs felt like polished ivory.

It was about time for a telephone to ring or a door bell's clamor. Instead there was nothing but soft night air and astral music. I drew back for breath and said, "One thing—was this your idea or your analyst's?"

A hand faster than a cobra slapped the side of my face, not hard, not gently. "Bastard," she breathed. "Call the prescription my own." She sagged against me, I bent over and lifted her behind the knees. As I carried her into the house her head fell back over the edge of my arm, the lashes fluttered and her eyes closed. They were long lashes, like tiny Japanese fans. Her hair fell back from a perfect widow's peak and her lips looked hot and swollen. Her thighs tautened and I heard her shoes hit the floor.

From the living room I could see an open door; a bedroom with a poster bed and a quilted coverlet. When I lowered her onto it she opened her eyes, laughed suddenly and arched her back.

The blouse was the first to come off, then her bra. Lacing her fingers behind her head, she murmured lazily, "The rest is up to you."

CHAPTER SEVEN

When I left it was something before midnight and Alma was deeply asleep. Setting the door catch, I stepped out groggily and began walking toward where I had left the Olds. It seemed that I had left it farther away than I had remembered. Unlocking it, I sank behind the wheel, shook myself and blinked. I was beat. Alma had provided more surprises than a novelty catalogue. Alma—the doll that had ritzed me to a husk the evening before. I couldn't credit myself for the whole enterprise, John Barleycorn deserved his due. My lips were dry, my mouth seemed coated with ashes. Opening the glove compartment, I pulled out a gourd of Teacher's and unscrewed the metal cap. I didn't drink a lot—just enough to drag me back to reality. Enough to orient myself. I was parked on Volta Place, Georgetown, District of Columbia, U.S.A. It seemed commonplace after the planets we had been exploring.

Now that my thirst was quenched I realized that I was hungry. I could feel my spine through my stomach. Really hungry. Hungry enough to eat roast polar bear and pick my teeth with the claws. Starting the engine, I idled back to Wisconsin and down to M Street. There was a terrace table at France's, low-pitch lighting and a menu that seemed more than adequate. I ordered the sirloin warmed slightly, salad with a kiss of garlic, and a brace of highballs.

By the time the steak arrived I was indifferent to worldly cares. There was a gentle humming in my ears and a glow on my face. Around twelve-thirty I paid my check and tottered out to my car. A corsage of pansies fluttered by in pipestem chinos, black open-throat shirts, scraggly beards and trailing the scent of Bois des Isles. Their high-pitched chatter reminded me of an aviary. Four angelinas out purchasing a quart of highdive to liven up their pad. Georgetown. I started the engine and drove away.

Not far from the apartment I found myself nodding. I turned on the radio and listened to records until I had to concentrate on driving down the ramp to the basement garage. Braking the Olds, I let the engine idle, waiting for Barney to come out of the office and do the parking chore. No Barney. Shrugging, I slid the car back into gear and backed into a slot. Then I turned off the ignition and got out. Barney was probably dozing at his desk. I was walking toward the office to hang up my keys when I noticed that his desk light was out. Halting, I called for Barney, then walked ahead. Probably the bulb had burned out and he was scaring up a new one.

As a decision it was a poor one, based only on superficial evidence. If I had been less foggy I might have sensed danger and taken the warning. Instead, I walked on into the office and groped for the key board. Behind me I heard someone chuckle faintly. I began to whip around but it was too late. Far too late for that. Someone had kicked the props from a deadfall and it slammed into the back of my head. As I dropped forward across the desk my last thought was for the keys that had fallen from my hand. Then, nothing at all.

The first identifiable sensations were that I had crossed the continent several times: through the heat of Death Valley, through Montana snows and rivers surging with flood crests. All that travel had made me infinitely tired. Pain grew like a sunburst, filling my partly conscious world. I tried to shout but all I heard was a groan.

I tried again and felt sick. My stomach rolled over and I retched. Nothing else happened. Then a sneering laugh. A harsh voice said, "He's waking up. Christ, I thought you finished him."

I opened my eyes.

I had to shut them because a light was shining directly at me. My hands moved, searched, and felt the seat and arms of a chair. I was sprawled in a chair like a party drunk. A wooden chair with hard rungs. Fingers opened one of my eyes, a hand hit the side of my face, rocking me. "You slept long enough, lover-boy," a voice rasped. "It's time to talk."

My heels dug into carpet and pushed me upright. I lifted one hand to shield my eyes and opened them.

The light came from a desk. Behind it sat two or three men. All I could see were their hands and arms. By turning my head slightly I could avoid the light's direct glare. Standing a yard away was a man in a powder-blue suit. He was a short thick man with hands like luncheon hams. The hair on them was so black it was almost blue. His face was round and scarred. His ears looked as though panthers had chewed them and he was nearly bald. A man over forty with a gold tooth in his lower jaw. The rest of his teeth were the color of tobacco juice. His oversized coat hung smoothly from his shoulders but not so smoothly I couldn't see the butt of a gun tucked high under his left armpit. Every time I breathed a bolt of pain shot through my head, jarring me when it bounced back from the inside of my skull. I wet my lips and tried to look intelligent.

Baldy said, "You took your sweet time, lover-boy. You always sleep late?"

"Depends on the company."

From behind the desk someone laughed. Not a pleasant sound; the way embalmers laugh when a corpse cuts up. I struggled upright and gripped the chair arms. "What happened to Barney?" I croaked.

"The trouble you're in and you worry about the night watchman," Baldy jeered. "Let's say he was takin' a snooze."

"You said something about trouble."

Baldy edged closer. "That was the word—unless raping and killing a girl ain't trouble from where you come from."

I laughed shortly. Even that hurt. "So I killed her. That figures. Where do we go from there?"

On the desk a hand pushed forward a piece of paper. A different, crisper voice said, "You sign this. Then you walk out."

"I'll bet," I grated. "I can see myself going out of here. Two guys on my shoulders and my toes marking up the rug."

The new voice took on an edge of menace. "Suit yourself, Bentley. Sign this and argue with the cops later—or don't sign it and end up on the river bottom with rocks in your pockets."

I tried to square my shoulders and look tough. "That's where I'm headed anyway. Why make it easier for you?"

From the corner of my eye I saw Baldy's hand lash out. It hit my cheekbone, almost knocking me out of the chair. Dizzily I caught my balance and saw the barrel of a gun staring at me. It looked like a Cyclops' eye, hard and empty. Peering up at Baldy, I shivered. He was looking at me as if I were already dead.

The barrel of the gun drifted sideways. He was getting ready to pistol-whip me. I held up one hand. "I'll sign," I croaked. "I'm no hero."

A tolerant chuckle from the darkness behind the desk. A manicured hand pushed the paper toward me, added a pen. The voice said, "Let him walk."

Gritting my teeth, I forced myself up and wavered to the desk. Bracing my hands on it, I peered down at the sheet of paper.

It was neatly typed and dated. It told how I had tried to force myself on one Loris Bolac, been repulsed, and how I had tied her, then raped and strangled her. A hand held the pen toward me. I leered at it and moved my hand. But not toward the pen.

Instead, my hand hit the base of the lamp, spinning it around. Sudden light showed three startled faces: Larry Zellerhaus, Senator Quinby and Lester Nagle. Then it crashed against the floor and the room was dark. Men were shouting.

A pistol barked beside me but by then I was on the floor and the muzzle flash told me where Baldy stood. From a crouch

I lunged at him. My head hit his breadbasket and my left hand clawed for the pistol. As we went over I heard air whistle out of his lungs. His head hit hard and he yelped. I heard the pistol clatter away. Rolling free, I scrambled for it as the ceiling light went on.

"*Hold it!*" someone shouted.

Picking myself up, I turned slowly around.

Larry Zellerhaus had a revolver in his hand. Not a big one, a .38 hammerless. A stocking gun. But big enough to leave an exit hole in me the size of a canteloupe. I went rigid.

"Up with them," he barked. "Don't move a hair."

Baldy was picking himself up slowly. His mouth was twisted in pain and his eyes were wild. His breathing came in short gasps. His hands clasped his thorax and he gave me a murderous glance. Then he turned and grabbed his pistol. I was panting hard. If my head hurt I wasn't noticing it. I was watching Baldy. He turned around and I heard the safety snick off. "In the belly," he screamed. "One in the belly and I'm gonna love it!"

From behind me a voice said coolly, "You'll put away the heat before it's shot out of your hand." A new voice.

Baldy's face paled. His lips moved but no sound came. Slowly his gun hand lowered. Just as slowly I turned and saw two men in the doorway. One man was tall and dark-haired with a light scar under one eye. For a gunman he was handsome. The man beside him was shorter and as lean as a shadow. He was the man who had spoken. As I turned, his eyes left Baldy and moved to me. His right hand lifted and fell in a gesture of disgust. The ceiling light showed his pain-ravaged face, the well-tailored drape of his shoulders. Maury Renzo said, "What's this, Bentley?"

"Parlor games," I husked. "Who killed Loris Bolac. These gentlemen seemed to think I should confess to it." I shrugged. "We differed."

In lockstep the two men came nearer. Like a falcon on a perch Maury Renzo stared at Zellerhaus. After a while he spat on the carpet. "Bungler," he said and cursed him. Then he faced

Quinby. "Get out," he snarled. "Get out and take that panz with you."

Through all this Senator Quinby and Nagle had done nothing except shrink out of the way. Quinby began to splutter, then the sound died away. Nagle's face was as white as polished bone.

As they began to file out of the door Maury Renzo rasped, "You do what you're told and only that. You take no initiative and you develop no ideas. Is that understood?"

Quinby halted and turned. "Yes, Maury," he said hoarsely.

"See that you don't forget it. This one could have been fatal."

They almost stumbled over each other getting out. I lifted one hand to my cheekbone and took it away. No blood. On the credit side of the ledger. Maury Renzo moved his head curtly, his bodyguard left his side and bore down on Baldy. Baldy shrank away from him but not soon enough. The tall man feinted with his pistol hand, then pistoned his left into Baldy's midriff. Baldy yelped and jackknifed over, both hands clawing at his belly. The tall man chuckled, then straightened him with another left. Baldy went over backward, as limp as noonday wash. The tall man licked the knuckles of his left hand and strode back beside Maury Renzo. On the round Zellerhaus face were patches of white. He licked his lips and laid his revolver on the table.

Maury Renzo was staring at him again. He cursed him once more and said, "What in God's name did you hope to accomplish by this?"

Zellerhaus sat down in a chair. He lifted one arm helplessly and tried to avoid Renzo's gaze. "Someone killed Peachy, Maury, you know that. Until the murder's solved the Senator's on the hook. This guy looked like a natural. Hell, it seemed simple."

With shriveling scorn Maury Renzo said, "When I bought you I was supposed to be buying brains. What I bought was a maggoty manure heap. You were supposed to be the smartest fixer in Washington." He took two steps toward Zellerhaus and whipped the back of his hand against the lobbyist's mouth.

The sound was wet and crunchy. Zellerhaus howled and rocked back. Blood rolled from his split lip. Maury Renzo snorted, "Washington isn't supposed to be my town, it's supposed to be yours. But I can tell you one thing about it: kill Bentley and every Metropolitan cop will work eighty hours a week until the killer burns. That much I know."

"Thanks, Maury," I wheezed.

His head turned slowly. For him a lot of color showed in his face. It looked almost like flesh. "For what? This comes under the heading of self-protection."

Zellerhaus drew one hand away from his injured mouth. "How was I supposed to know?" he complained. "Jesus Christ, Maury. I thought he was just a snooper who lived next door."

"I pay you to know everything," Maury said in a glacial voice. "You have any thoughts about anything, you tell me. Understand? If I didn't need you I'd have had you shot just now. Think of that the next time you're considering any kind of independent action."

"Sure, Maury," Zellerhaus gabbled. "Sure. Anything you say."

Beside Maury Renzo the tall bodyguard's face was as deadpan as cast bronze. His pistol covered Zellerhaus unwaveringly.

"Put it away," Maury Renzo snapped, and the pistol dropped out of sight.

To me he said, "Need any help, Bentley?"

"I can make it," I said and stumbled toward the door. As I passed into a dark hallway I heard them walking after me. "This way," Renzo called and I heard a door open. Turning back, I saw him waiting at the doorway. "Car?" he asked.

"I guess they must have driven me."

"You'll go in mine. I'm not through with Zellerhaus." Turning, he snapped an order at his bodyguard. The tall man loped down the steps and disappeared. Heavily Maury Renzo said, "He'll take you home."

"That'll be a help," I said. "Sometimes this far out cabs are a little hard to hail."

He had been looking away from me. Now his face turned and he said, "You thinking of making a big thing of this?"

"I'm making nothing of it."

He nodded. Then: "Any thoughts about anything?"

"Maybe you'd have been better off gunning Zellerhaus tonight."

"Why?"

"Whatever scared the Senator and Zellerhaus is still around to scare them. Together they haven't the guts of a bull minnow. If one of them killed Peachy—or had her killed—it'll come out in time. How far you're tied into it I don't know. But their kind likes company. Particularly walking the Last Mile."

"You think I had her killed?" he said dully.

"No," I said. "Not that there isn't other blood on your hands. If you'd known there was a problem concerning Peachy you'd have handled it differently. She'd be alive today, though not necessarily in this country."

He nodded slowly. "Thanks for giving me that. And for what it's worth I know only that she got herself killed. She was Larry's doll for a while, then he wanted a change. Quinby wanted to take her over. I okayed it. It seemed the easiest solution. You knew her well?"

"Hardly at all."

"Not my style," Maury Renzo said. "I didn't know she was living next to you, they don't tell me details like that. To Zellerhaus it wouldn't have made any difference. To me it would." He shook his head. "What a lot of brains I buy with my dirty dollars."

A car purred up to the steps. I glanced down and saw a black Lincoln town car. Overhead there was only a thin slice of moon but it made the Lincoln's black lacquer glint like oiled opal.

Renzo gestured toward it. I started down the steps. Somewhere in distance a dog barked. Coon and possum country. Fox country, too. For some. I opened the well-oiled rear door, got in and glanced up at the Zellerhaus manor. Outside, Stratford-on-Avon architecture with probably no more than seven bedrooms and a kitchen big enough to feed a Marine regiment without crowding. Carefully trimmed shrubbery and symmetrical blue spruces, slim as missiles pointing at the tissue moon. A patch of clouds blotted it out and when I looked back Maury Renzo was gone and the Lincoln was sliding down the curving drive. Without looking back, the driver said, "When Maury's feeling democratic he sits up front here with me."

"He may have some reason to trust you."

The voice thickened. "That ain't nice, pal. I don't take that so good."

"Oh, Christ," I said wearily, "try to think how little I might care."

He grunted. After a while he said, "I don't figure it. A jasper like you being a friend of Maury's."

"Mr. Renzo to you. And I wouldn't say we were friends."

"He don't stick his neck out but once in a long century, pal. You must rate."

I stared out at the dark border of trees. The road dipped and wound down and the Lincoln sped over Chain Bridge. At a traffic light on the District side he half turned and drawled, "I heard of you before, Bentley. Two guys had the job I got now. I heard you opened up the slot. I oughta thank you."

"You're welcome."

He peered up at the signal light and looked back again. "I also hear you handle a rod pretty good. Colt?"

I shook my head. "Walther P thirty-eight. Nine millimeter."

The light flashed green. He slid the clutch into gear and the Lincoln shot ahead like a greased piston. Closing my eyes, I fought back a surge of pain. The gunman's voice said casually, "I'm pretty good myself. We oughta have a shoot-out one day."

"Dummy targets?" I rasped. "Or just the two of us?"

Under the flash of the street light his face was harder than tungsten steel. "Never can tell, pal," came his tight voice. "You sure never can tell."

CHAPTER EIGHT

Another day. An ice poultice had reduced most of the facial swelling and a handful of aspirin was keeping skull pain at a low throb. I managed a feeble swagger as I went into Kellaway's office but it was lost on him. When the door shut he grunted but kept on at what he was doing. He was at the window, bent over, injecting something around the roots of his dwarf tree. He withdrew the hypodermic syringe delicately, examined the barrel and wiped off the needle. Then he looked around. When he saw me he grunted again, strolled over to his desk and sat down. It was only ten-thirty but the office was steaming like a Turkish bath.

I fitted myself into a chair and said, "Fine police protection when a fellow gets cold-calked in the garage of his own apartment."

His eyes were heavy with fatigue but they opened a little wider. "You interest me mildly. Care to put out some details or is this one of your whimsical days?"

I tried a cigarette but it tasted like the city dump. I flicked it into the shiny spittoon and told him what had happened to me the night before. All except the preliminary hours with Alma.

While I was telling him his eyes narrowed. Otherwise, not a muscle moved. When I stopped he said, "Making any charges?"

"It happened in another jurisdiction," I said. "Anyway, I'd have a fat chance proving anything against a U.S. Senator, without witnesses."

"Even less than that. The way the ball bounces around here."

"Quinby didn't lay a finger on me. Nor Zellerhaus. Only Baldy."

"If you're interested you can check the mug files. With that gold tooth Baldy oughta be an easy make."

"I'll see him again," I said moodily. "Probably in the not-distant future. I'll remember him."

"Junkie?"

"He didn't confide in me."

His hand brushed away nonexistent smoke. "So why tell me your troubles?"

I leaned forward, propped my elbows on the desk and gazed at him admiringly. "A friend is a friend. Some fellows can only write Dear Abby or Dorothy Dix. Me, I know a big fellow who's a full Captain in the Metropolitan Police. Between hopping up his dwarf tree and killing traffic tickets for politicians he listens to me. Believe me, it gives me a warm glow all over. Guess I'm just lucky."

He studied me balefully. Finally he jerked out a cigar and lighted it. When it was going, he said, "Okay, so I had it coming. What do you figure I can do?"

"Not much." I sat back in the chair. "I'm taking my lumps like the little stalwart I am. Hell, I asked for them."

"That's the truth. You say the Nagle lad is a ringtail?"

"If I know the breed."

"Maybe the Senator keeps him around for odd Fridays." Kellaway cackled and dropped ash on the rug.

"Anything's possible. Remember the New England Senator who got caught in a daisy chain?"

"And not many years back. But Quinby kept the Bolac piece."

"She was lent by Zellerhaus, expenses paid. Charming how the influence-peddlers get what they want."

"It's nothing new," he said sourly. "They did it in Rome when Caesar was mayor. They'll be doing it when we're parceling out beach frontage on the moon." He stared at his thumbnail.

A plainclothesman came in, coughed, bent over and whispered a message to Kellaway. Kellaway dismissed him and went on staring at his thumbnail. After a while he said, "This morning we let Ray Stroud go. There were two guys to say he was playing knock rummy with them at the time Loris Bolac was being strangled." He gnawed a hangnail.

"Could Ray stagger out or hadn't you really had time to work him over?"

"Maybe he was pushed around a little. Hell, Stroud had the picture frame. His own damn fault."

"Sure," I said. "And the citizen who gets in the way when a cop's gunning a fugitive, it's his fault, too. Tough luck. But the family shouldn't mind. Hell, the City stands the burial costs. What more do you want from a benevolent City?"

He withdrew the cigar from his mouth, rewound a leaf end that had soaked loose and looked at me. "I'm too old and too tired to get all fretted because you got yourself busted on the head last night. Nobody asked you to include yourself in this Bolac case. You'll keep poking around, getting mixed up in things that are police business, and one day someone smarter than you—or maybe just only a little faster with a gun and not smart at all— will end your poking days. We've had this out before so I know it's useless. I mention it only for the record."

"This time there's one slight difference, Captain. I didn't include myself in this case. I haven't done one thing anybody could take umbrage at. All I did was have the misfortune to occupy an apartment next door to where a girl got murdered. Last night's gang was looking for a patsy to frame and they selected me. They've been told off, by high authority, so that's not likely to happen again, but the killer's still at large. Unless you think Peachy raped herself and garroted herself out of remorse."

A long cloud of gray smoke was his answer. His eyes flickered. After a while he said, "Don't you worry about the killer being at large. We'll get him. Maybe not this afternoon, but we'll lay him by the heels. I wasn't prepared to say so yesterday, but Quinby's fingerprints were found inside her apartment."

"Big news. Whose prints were on her beautiful white body?"

He ignored it with another cloud of smoke. I coughed and leaned aside. He said, "Other prints showed up, too. Some by a fellow named Redpath, a lawyer. Still others we haven't identified."

"How did you identify Redpath's."

"Civil Service files."

"I thought you said he was a lawyer."

"A guy can be a lawyer and Civil Service both."

"Whereabouts in Civil Service?" I was beginning to enjoy it. "Don't tell me he's a Senate page?"

He looked uncomfortable. "Just where Redpath works happens to be my business and not yours." He glanced at his watch. "Redpath's due here not long from now."

I pushed out of the chair and adjusted my wrinkled suit. "So long as you've got him here you might ask him why he doesn't divorce his wife—Alma Ward, you know." Turning I headed for the door. Behind me Kellaway snarled, "You double-crossing son of a bitch!"

"Never underrate the amateurs," I called sweetly. "Mutual confidence can be a wonderful thing."

It was eleven o'clock when I pushed into the office and met Mrs. Bross's disapproving stare. All she said was, "Phone messages on your desk," and let me pass without a lecture on late hours and loose living.

One message was from Mrs. Jeanette Ward, the other from her humanized daughter. To establish priority I flipped a coin. It came out the old lady so I sat down and dialed the District Detective Agency. When the receptionist answered I asked for Artie Von Amond. His voice was depressingly chipper so I cut him off by telling him I wanted biographic data on Quinby, Nagle and Zellerhaus.

"Not gonna be any too damn easy to check on any of them."

"Right. And I don't want credit-rating stuff. What I want is the sort of juicy tidbits a newspaper morgue isn't likely to hold."

"But police files would. Hell, you can get that stuff from Kellaway. Or aren't you speaking this week?"

"Barely."

"Anything else I ought to know?"

"It's the Loris Bolac murder," I muttered. "The blonde with the nylons around her throat."

"Yeah? What's your interest, Steve?"

"She was a neighbor. Let it go at that."

"I guess I have to. This may take a couple of days."

"Not if you put enough men on it."

"Yeah. I'll call when I have something. Anything else?"

"How'd you feel about putting a tail on Quinby?"

"I wouldn't like it. Too easy a way to get my license lifted. Sorry."

"Do what you can then." I hung up and searched the phone book for Senator Quinby's number. It wasn't listed. Dialing the Senate Office Building I asked for the chambers of Senator Quinby. A twangy female voice told me boredly that the Senator was back home. No, she had no idea when the Senator might return.

"Darn it," I said. "I have something to deliver personally to the Senator."

"You may leave it here."

"I'd prefer leaving it at his home."

She thought it over. "Something large?"

"In a way. But the parcel isn't much bigger than an ordinary envelope."

Hurriedly she said, "I think I understand, but you shouldn't say things like that by telephone. Someone might be listening."

"Good heavens. Are you serious, ma'am?"

"I'm afraid so," she said loftily, and gave me an apartment address on upper Connecticut Avenue. I thanked her humbly and hung up. Making a note of the address, I put it in my pocket.

Then I called Mrs. Jeanette Ward.

The maid answered and there was an interval while a telephone was carried out to the conservatory and plugged in. Then I heard a voice as sharp as flaked flint. "You took your time returning my call, young man."

"Sorry, Mrs. Ward. As I explained to you yesterday, things come up that have to be taken care of. But you were high on my list."

"I don't believe you. I think you're a late sleeper. Country didn't get built by late sleepers. Got built by men who were up and about their business at dawn."

"True enough. Maybe I'm suffering from low blood pressure or leukemia. There ought to be an organic explanation for this dragged-out feeling. Sometimes it's overpowering."

She humphed at that and I thought I heard her stick drum the floor irritably. Then she said, "Well, have you made up your mind?"

"About what, Mrs. Ward?"

"About the offer I made you yesterday, you young idiot. What else have we got to talk about?"

"I thought the offer was withdrawn—after I'd so cleverly seen its ulterior motives."

"Nonsense. I want you on my payroll. Well, what about it?"

I lowered my voice slightly and said, "Sincerely, Mrs. Ward, your offer is about the most complimentary thing I've had happen in years and I'm grateful beyond anything you might imagine. But yesterday I told you my reasons against it. They still hold. They always will."

When she spoke again her tone was almost maternal. "Well, I must say I'm not accustomed to being refused. If it was a question of money you would have said so, I suppose."

"Yes."

"Then I can only wish you luck. And wish that I had known you before you became so damned independent."

"Thank you. But that would have been long ago."

"I'm close to a century old," she sniffed. "Now that's disposed of, however unsatisfactorily to me, I think you should know that my daughter shared brunch with me an hour ago and had some highly flattering things to say about you."

I said nothing.

When she got tired of waiting, she said, "Young man, are you making love to my daughter?"

"That's something you'll have to take up with Alma."

I thought I heard a chuckle, but the sound was distant and faint as though it might have been strained through a lace hand-kerchief. Then I heard her voice again: "In my opinion it would do her good. A great deal of good. Good morning, sir."

"Adios, Mrs. Ward."

I replaced the phone, stared at it and began to laugh. The old bawd, I thought. Vicarious fun at her age.

When I had had my little laugh I searched the directory for Alma's number and called her. A maid with a German accent told me that Miss Ward was at her office and supplied me the number. I dialed it and two secretaries later Alma was speaking to me. Her voice was low and cool as a mint frappé. "Wretch, you abandoned me last night."

"I could hardly compromise you with the servants. Unless they're accustomed to all-night guests."

"That's terribly unfunny," she said shakily. "I thought you might be interested enough to call me. Or is a one-night stand your limit?"

"That's something we might discuss on another occasion, beautiful. Surrounded by the scent of jasmine and floating on scotch mist."

"You make it sound awfully tempting. Sorry, but jasmine won't do a thing until nightfall. I was thinking of something more proximate."

"Lunch, possibly?"

"You practically made me ask you. I can see we're in for a fine time of it, Steven." Her voice held a trace of annoyance, a trace of disillusion.

"Cheer up, pigeon. Meet me at the Colmenar at one. You can tell your snooty friends I'm just a TV technician."

"Suppose I do no explaining at all?" she bridled.

"Then be your folly on your own head."

"As it has always been." I could have heard a kiss breathed over the wire or it could have been just static. Then the phone clicked off and I heaved a sigh.

Mrs. Bross poked her head in and said, "How are you feeling?"

"As frayed as an old tow rope."

Her eyes narrowed. "Mr. Bentley, did you get in a fight last night?"

"I never landed a blow."

Her lips pursed. "That isn't like you, Mr. Bentley."

"I'm not as young as I used to be. Lend me three aspirin and a glass of water and I'll work two hours without stopping."

That brought a grim smile to her lips. She disappeared and came back with what I needed. When I had gulped it down I said, "If Artie Von Amond calls later, tell him I'm lunching at the Colmenar."

"I might have known," she sniffed. "A redhead this time?"

"Uh-uh. Hair as black as a raven. Skin coppery-gold and a figure like a Paris model. Except bustier. Considerably."

Color spotted her cheeks. "Single, Mr. Bentley?"

"They never are. Not when they come like that. Now be off with you."

Enough work had piled up to hold me there past dinner. I cleared away as much as I could and cabbed over to the Colmenar a few minutes before one. The basement bar was quiet and cool and dim, with not too much smoke or loud chatter. Trouble was it didn't open until evening. The headwaiter ushered me to a wall table and issued me a menu the size of a pup tent. I didn't bother to decipher it. A waiter in striped pants, a chartreuse, double-breasted jacket and a stiff-bosom shirt was drifting by so I called him over. He had smooth olive skin, almond eyes and ringlets of curly hair. Also a nervous mouth and a hunted look. The Colmenar was maintaining its reputed personnel standards.

From him I ordered enough scotch, ice and soda to hold two people for half an hour. Then I lighted a cigarette and fingered the bump behind my head. Still painful enough to rule out hats for another week. When my do-it-yourself kit arrived I built a sturdy drink and dived in. By the time I came up for air people were arriving and the headwaiter was busier than a widow at a wake. The way he flew through the air, his coattails might take a permanent set.

Then, not more than ten minutes after the appointed hour, Alma Ward came in.

CHAPTER NINE

The headwaiter bowed her all the way over to my table as though she were the Ranee of Dawpur. And all Alma gave him was an offhand freeze. Hell, she was old Thurston Ward's daughter as well as a celebrity in her own right. I let the headwaiter pull out the table and seat her beside me. His hands were fluttering like moths in mortal combat. As she plucked off her gloves she hissed, "Don't you rise when a lady's being seated?"

"Depends on how well I know her. Hungry?"

"Not very." She picked up an amber jigger and poured herself a drink. Sipping it she glanced at my face and frowned. "Were you *that* carried away last night?"

"Oh, the bruises? That came slightly later. A short fat man with a thick gun struck me down and carted me off to Fairfax County. To a big estate set back in the pines. By daylight it's quite a spread. The moon didn't show much of it last night. Besides, I was mostly in a room with four men. Me staring into a spotlight."

"You were *what?*" The drink banged down on the table hard enough to rattle the silver.

I told her the rest. She listened, wincing occasionally, and by the time I had finished, her hand was clinging to my arm.

"Poor baby," she murmured. "It must have been absolute hell. What are you going to do about it?"

"What would be your idea of something to do?"

"Tell the police—bring charges, of course."

I patted her hand. "Look, angel," I said patiently, "I'm only a night-school lawyer but I know enough about false arrest and slander to know I'd need a pair of pretty convincing witnesses to make a story as outlandish as that stick."

"They kidnaped you and transported you across a state line. That's FBI business."

"What isn't? If I told J. Edgar himself the same tale I told you he'd say the same thing: boy, you need witnesses."

Lifting her glass, she drank what looked like a lot. It seemed too bad we weren't back in the old walled garden, all wound up in each other's arms and nibbling like crazy. Her lips were set in a determined line. "It isn't something I plan to forget. It'll be featured in the final exposé. You can count on it, darling."

"Not if you care for me, it won't," I said. "What I told you was for your pearly ears alone. And only to give you a slight idea of the kind of thing this is turning out to be. I told you before that this was a hard town. It is. Behind the glittering diplomatic façade and the simpering sanctimoniousness it's a dirty gutter, as tough as anything north of 98th Street in New York."

"You really believe that, Steve?" she said doubtfully.

"I've learned it," I said harshly. "I learned it early and I learned it late. I don't blame the cops and I don't entirely blame the people. It's too much money scraping against too much misery. Hand-wringing doesn't help either, it's only a cover-up. The problem's more basic. You've spent part of your adult life here. Surely you can't be entirely innocent of what goes on."

Her lashes lowered. "Maybe I just don't want to think about it, admit it."

"That's the average reaction. You're out after Quinby and Zellerhaus, sure. As individuals, and because they're important enough to rate national coverage. But what about the muggers and the heroin-pushers and the white-slavers and the faggotry? Is it the volume that appalls or is it just too tawdry to touch? This town needs a purifying rain, and every week it's postponed enlarges the need."

Quietly she said, "You're right. Only I'm not a social reformer, a cocktail party do-gooder. Little as you know me you must realize that. The job you're talking about will have to be done by someone tougher and more dedicated than me. There, that's my confession for the day. Does it change anything?"

"No," I said grumpily. "Even the setting's against me." I lifted my glass and touched it to hers. She breathed a kiss across the rim and smiled meltingly. So much for that.

The headwaiter had glided back with a basket of interesting luncheon suggestions. Alma ordered a salad bowl and a plate of Ry-Krisp. I asked for lamb chops, shoestring potatoes and garden vegetables. The headwaiter's face fell. He had figured us for flaming swords and Swedish pancakes soaked in Cointreau and we had let him down. I felt I should grip his hand and sob for forgiveness. Instead I let him coast away and organized two new drinks.

Lifting mine, I said, "Your mother phoned a while back. Among other things she inquired if I'd been making love to you."

"Did she?" Her cheeks colored slightly.

"She did. Apparently the thought arose following a breakfast conversation with you."

"Brunch," she corrected. "I must have been indiscreet. Do you mind?"

"I suppose not. And your mother may get a kick out of thinking about it. Between the two of you the days are filled with surprises."

Her hand turned her glass slowly. In an offhand voice she said, "I didn't mean to give away our little secret, Steve. On the other hand I'm sure it doesn't shock her. For twenty years before his death my father maintained a number of ladies in fashionable circumstances and mother adjusted her life accordingly. Mother wanted to hire you. What did you say?"

"I thanked her for the compliment and told her I couldn't."

"I'm sorry."

"Not really. If I were under Ward control you'd lose any interest you have in me."

She lowered her glass and stared at it. "I suppose you're right. We're accustomed to buying what we want. In your case I thought a second try might be worthwhile. Subconsciously I must need a defense against you."

"Thanks." I grinned. "You make me feel like the Second Most Dangerous Man in London, with veiled lady callers, perfumed cachets and midnight trysts with headstrong duchesses."

"Profligate. Do you know anything else about the supposed murderer of Peachy?"

"Stroud was released this morning."

"Why?"

"The usual reason: an alibi plus witnesses." I sipped my drink. "Leaving the police back where they started. Except for one thing I might as well tell you: they found your husband's fingerprints in Angel Eyes' apartment."

She looked up quickly, then glanced away. In a low voice she said, "I'm not really surprised. And I'm not hypocrite enough to censure him. Jay would be attracted to her type—cheap and available. I can't help feeling a little disillusioned, though. I thought living with me might have taught him something."

"Maybe it did."

Her face turned back and she said tightly, "Such as?"

"That a man can top his class in law school and be a bust in the bedroom."

The tip of her tongue flicked across her lips.

"Or," I went on, "that the male ought to wear the pants and pay the bills."

"This is the twentieth century, Steve. Women vote, practice medicine, even run big businesses. Or haven't you heard?"

"And every year the divorce rate zooms. Nothing rounds out a home like a log fire, a faithful dog and a wife who's not too proud to fetch her husband's pipe and slippers."

"You're almost antique," she said haughtily. "I suppose you'd have me making peach preserves as well."

Reaching across the table, I pinched her cheek lightly. "Not you, gorgeous. But then we aren't planning on setting up a little home."

Her eyes fell away. Lifting her glass, she downed the rest of her drink and dabbed her lips.

"Tell me one thing—did Jay get involved with Peachy for simple sex reasons or did he cultivate her because she was Quinby's doll?" I asked.

"He didn't confide in me."

"I'll bet he didn't. Anyway, here he comes now."

Her eyes widened and together we watched Jay Redpath threading among the tables toward us. His face was paler than yesterday and he looked mad. He nearly collided with a bus boy but he kept on coming. He jabbed stiff fingers onto the table and grated, "I saw your car outside, Alma. I didn't know this fellow would be here."

"This fellow is here by prior appointment," I said. "On the other hand a man has a right to talk with his wife. I'll dust off if no one objects."

His face was ugly. "I wanted to see you, too, Bentley. Yesterday you said my little secret was safe with you. So this morning the police ask me to stop by. That makes you a liar."

I could feel my face getting hot. "Easy, boy. I don't have to make any explanations to you, but whatever the police may have learned about you and Peachy didn't come from me."

"No?" he sneered. "Then I suppose—"

Levelly Alma said, "Your fingerprints, Jay." Her voice lifted. "It's your own fault, so don't blame Steve. I hope your shabby little dalliance was richly satisfying."

His face grew even paler. "I see," he said in a deadly voice. "Thanks for letting me know how things stand." He squared his shoulders and bent over toward me. "I ought to break your jaw,

Bentley. I don't know what your game is but I'm telling you to stay away from my wife."

Anxiously Alma said, "Jay! Don't make a scene."

"Why not?" he said with a sickly smile. "Why shouldn't I? I'm nobody important. Nobody bothers about me. I'm only Jay Redpath. Who the hell cares what I do? If I were someone as important as Alma Ward it might make a difference." His body seemed to slump. He wiped the back of his hand across his mouth.

Alma's voice was steely. "Good-by, Jay."

He glanced at her and laughed nastily. "Good-by, Jay," he repeated. "Pick up your toys and run along home. Thanks, Alma. I'll remember that. I'll remember it a long time."

Other than his echoing voice the big room was devoid of sound. Waiters had halted in their tracks. The entire attention of fifty diners was focused on our table. Around my neck my collar was getting tight.

Alma's eyes were fixed on Jay's. "I said good-by," she repeated coldly.

Abruptly he whirled and took off through the maze of tables. A fork clattered against the floor. Off in the distance the head-waiter was gnawing his bundle of menus.

I said, "This happen often?"

She shrugged. "From time to time. Jay isn't very mature, I'm afraid." Her voice was a little hollow, with possibly a tinge of self-indictment.

"He looks fairly normal to me. The tableau isn't one I'd enjoy discovering if I were in his place."

"What does he expect?" she said icily and splashed scotch into her glass. "He shouldn't have married me."

"Or you shouldn't have let him."

She glanced at me sharply. "I'm to blame, too?"

"You treat him like a muddy puppy. How long is a man supposed to absorb punishment like that?"

"As long as I say," she grated and lifted her glass.

Around us conversation resumed tentatively. Waiters broke into motion and I heard the snap of the headwaiter's fingers.

Sipping my drink, I gazed at her. "Well," I said, "I've seen how you dispatch a loved one. So when it's my turn for the big good-by there'll be no surprises."

Her hand touched my wrist gently. "Steve, don't make me feel like a praying mantis. Jay made the mistake of trying to domesticate me. Out of envy and his own inadequacy. I think you're wises than that."

"Anyway, the lesson isn't lost on me."

Two waiters arrived just then. They served our lunch with mechanical precision but I wasn't hungry any longer. I fooled around with my frilly lamb chops until Alma had finished her salad. The encounter with Jay had bothered her less than a rough fingernail.

As we left the room all motion seemed suspended again and I could hear hushed whispers. For all it meant to Alma she could have been orbiting a hundred miles above the Earth. The head-waiter bowed her out nervously with never a glance at me.

The big Riley was parked in front of the entrance under a shade tree. Nearby a metal sign sternly warned against parking there. Hell, that sort of thing was for the peons, not Alma Ward.

Opening the door for her, I helped her in. She fitted the ignition key into the lock and blew me a kiss. "Busy tonight?" she asked.

"Probably not."

Something moved across her face. "You'll let me know, won't you? This is no time to search your conscience."

"I just feel sorry for the guy," I said. "He couldn't make the grade with you, but few men could. That's no reason to mop the floor with him."

One eyebrow lifted and the Riley purred into life. "I'll handle Jay my own way. It has nothing to do with us. Will I see you later?"

"Very possibly," I said and watched the Riley slide away.

At the corner a patrolman was staring up at a robin perched on a maple branch. When I reached him I said, "Officer, that foreign car was parked illegally for nearly an hour."

His eyes lowered and filmed with frost. "Whaddaya know? Show it to me and I'll ticket it."

"That's what I thought," I said and moved on. A taxi stopped for me and I got in. As the cab moved across town I found myself wondering how deeply involved with Peachy Jay had been. Now that I had seen him in action I could imagine him falling for Peachy and trying to get her to break with Quinby. And just as clearly I could see her turning him down. I wondered if Redpath had come back later that night, managed to waken her and gone in. I wondered if he had raped her and twisted the stocking around her throat.

Someone had.

CHAPTER TEN

Senator Quinby's pad was just off upper Connecticut near Taft Bridge. A six-story apartment house on a circular drive laced with hydrangea and dogwood. A quiet, conservative neighborhood with still enough old families to offset the invasion of bureaucrats, lobbyists and flash money. I had been parked on the drive for nearly an hour, slumped behind the wheel of my Olds, alternating between pipe and cigarettes and trying to look like someone's husband waiting for someone else's maid. And there were plenty of maids in the neighborhood, strolling with prams under the tall arching elms. Most of them looked solid enough for extra duty as battering rams, but a couple could have been imports from Paris or Berkeley Square, with provocative mouths and bodies that defied camouflage by starched bosoms and bulky skirts. A cutie sauntered past, flashed me a liquid smile and drifted on. My compliments, ma'am. Some other time. Some evening when I haven't got a mind burdened with worldly cares.

Reaching outside the window I tapped out my pipe on the door handle and pocketed it. I wiped my forehead with a limp handkerchief and looked back at Quinby's doorway. He could be back in the mountain country and unavailable. Or he could be just lying doggo to avoid publicity. Since he had given his office the not-in-town message it was reasonable he had done the same with the apartment management. Not a very complex character, Quinby. Just Zellerhaus's tame coon. A simple, uncomplicated role, and profitable. There was always more than just a possibility that Quinby had killed Peachy Bolac, but I couldn't see him leaving her body there under circumstances which made it traceable to him. She had been Zellerhaus's plover once, and according to Maury Renzo Zellerhaus had tired of her and let Quinby move in. Or the story could have been different, with Peachy making the first move toward Quinby and Zellerhaus having to go along with it. Out of that could have come resentment, even jealousy by fat-face Larry. And like Quinby he would have a key to her apartment. Apparently Zellerhaus had been the prime mover of last night's snatch. He was passing it off as interest in saving Quinby, but he could have had other, more personal motives in finding a patsy. After the way Maury Renzo had blasted him I didn't think Zellerhaus would be after me again; at least not for the same reasons. I remembered Baldy's crazy eyes, the pain of his fists, and my hands began to itch. I wanted to lay my Walther across those fat cheeks a few times and listen to him yelp. Torpedoes were all the same: king of the ash pile with a gun in his hand; without one, just another loogan.

The bus pulled up to a stop and moved on. I hardly noticed it. My left leg was falling asleep. Twisting around to straighten it I saw a girl dart across the street. She had shoulder-length dark hair and long straight bangs that nearly touched her eyebrows. She wore tight blue denims, moccasins and a beige sweater with a floppy turtleneck. In ninety-degree heat. Either she was smuggling avocados or what jiggled under her sweater was real. Her face held a youthful sulky beauty despite the pasty whiteness of her skin. A hip chick. From her figure she could have been anywhere between thirteen and twenty but her eyes were old. They were wise eyes that had seen too much in too short a time and they reminded me of someone else I had known.

As she stepped up on the curb in front of my bumper I saw her stop uncertainly and dig the back of her left leg with the toe of her right shoe. Her lips looked dry. Her fingers were long and almost skinny. She stared up at the apartment building as though she were making up her mind. Then she glanced around. Her eyes caught mine and she started self-consciously. I stuck out my head and made my voice hard. "Got a connection, chick?"

It jolted her. Her eyes widened, her fingers opened and closed and she strolled over, trying to keep it casual.

A yard away she stopped. "Fuzz or pushin'?"

"Pot," I purred. "Cured and mellow. You dig?"

One hand jammed into a slash pocket and she came closer. "Blow or show." Her elfin face was taut as a mask.

"Lay some bread on me."

Her hand pulled the pocket inside out. "Later. This your stash?"

"I'm holding."

Her head tossed around and she stared up at the apartment. "Bread," she murmured thirstily. "There'll be bread enough."

"You bugged?"

"Bugged plenty." She looked back at me, still not entirely convinced.

"Like pot's the answer. Cuban. Sweet as sugar, sugar."

She glanced up at the apartment again. "Like he was a Jeez-o square. A cubist, man." She laughed but the sound chilled me. "Later. I gotta split. For bread, man."

"Slide, chick. I'm stashed."

Turning she crossed the sidewalk and angled into the entrance. My palms were sweating. I fumbled a cigarette and lighted it. A hip chick and a hophead. A disciple of Mary Juana. I had managed to convince her I was a pusher. She could have told otherwise, but when they've had a fix they don't discriminate too well.

Time passed. I lighted another cigarette and studied the apartment door. I wondered what was taking her so long to collect. Maybe she was working for it. With her it would be as casual as a cough.

Then a man crossed into my field of vision. A tall man with a twitching walk as though his hips had once been crushed. At the apartment entrance he turned and glanced nervously around. I bent over and got interested in the brake pedal. When I looked up he had gone. Lester Nagle, Quinby's trained seal. His coming could mean something or nothing. Nagle could be a viper, a kokomo or a gowhead. Plenty of nolas were. Drugs gave them something they lacked, let them feel superior to the rest of the race. Dream wax, Miss Emma, white mosquitoes. Take your pick, sucker. The thought dried my mouth.

She came half running, half skipping out of the entrance, heading for me like a pet kitten. Opening the other door she piled in and patted her trouser pocket. "Bread, man," she burbled.

"Show me."

Her fingers pried into her pocket and plucked out a roll of bills, none less than ten dollars. In all there must have been a couple of hundred bucks. She was breathing hard. Her eyes seemed flecked with gold. She pulled off two tens and laid them on the seat. Reaching over, I fingered them. "Crazy," I said. "Cool bread. For work?"

Her eyes flashed. "With a square? Get lost."

My hand passed over the bills and circled her left wrist. She didn't seem to notice. Her eyelids fluttered and went slack. Leaning closer, I said, "I knew Peachy."

"*Fuzz!*" she shrieked. "Filthy fuzz! Take your goddam paw off me, copper!"

"Sizzle down," I snarled, and yanked hard as she tried to scramble out of the door. "I'm no copper, I just knew Peachy. You'd be the kid sister."

Her eyes were slits in a pillowcase. Her mouth twisted like an animal's.

"Yell," I said. "Let's get the law over here. You'll have a stick or a roach on you. Christ, I can smell it in your hair."

That punched her hard. She jerked her wrist free and sat there breathing hard. She cursed me.

I said, "You've got hooks into Quinby. How much is he riding for?"

She called me a dirty name.

I slapped her face. Her eyes blinked, her tongue caressed her lips and she began to whimper.

"That's only a sample. What's the name?"

"Rox...Roxy," she managed. "How'd you dig me?"

"The eyes, baby. The eyes, the face and the figure. All from the same mold. Unique now because Peachy's gone. Quinby was keeping her, but that's well known. What else are you selling him?"

Her eyes went dull the way a hawk's does when it faces the sun. I wondered if she had sneaked a jolt up there, or if it was only a trick. I grabbed her arm and shook her. "Blow," I snapped. "Blow quick!"

It only made her giggle. Her eyes trailed down to my hand and back up to my face. It made me feel foolish. I let go. Slowly she waved a finger at me. "It was you all along?" she simpered. "You." Her eyes gathered me in and petted me. "For a square, not bad. So Peachy flipped for you. Like I never knew."

"Let's drop the beatnik gibber."

Her face grew clever. "Like you had a pad and some pot. We could dangle toes and slide way out. Way far out, man."

"Skid back to earth, Roxy. Besides Quinby, who figured in Peachy's hush life?"

"You," she repeated with an idiot smile. "You, fuzzy." Her fingers picked up the two tens on the seat and tucked them into her pocket. "Like I got some pot in my pad. We could beetle down and get frantic." She giggled again. The sound was getting wearing.

Reaching across her I pushed open the door. Her face turned, startled. She shook her head and drew her feet onto the seat, snuggling against the cushion. "Out, baby," I rasped. "No pot, no pad. Just fresh air. Dangle. You've got bread draped all over you. Cut out."

Her lips parted and she said huskily, "Cool. I'd work with you, man. The rest of the day like."

"Thanks for the compliment," I said savagely, lifted my right foot, planted it against her thigh and pushed hard. It sent her teetering into the street. Steadying herself on the fender she shot me a venomous glance and made an obscene gesture. I slammed the door. She shook herself and skipped across the street. When I looked back, she was slouching at the bus stop nibbling one finger. A sweet, unspoiled kid. Just the kind to trot home to mother. My hand was shaking as I filled my pipe. I let a lot of smoke circulate inside the car. A lot of smoke was needed to cut the scent of pot. Christ, she must have used it for shampoo.

A bus skidded to a stop and when I looked over again she was gone. Back to her pad for poetry, pot and jazz cooler than a deep freeze. All I had learned from her was that Peachy was dividing her favors with someone other than Quinby, who she didn't know. Or wouldn't say. Jay Redpath was a known candidate, but there could have been others, and probably were.

Nagle was up in Quinby's apartment. He could have been the payoff man if Quinby was really out of town. Or he could have gotten there after Roxy collected and never seen her. Either way Roxy's being able to collect only showed what I already knew— that Quinby had a horror of publicity. She didn't need anything else on him and she knew it. I wondered how long he'd be willing to pay. Or how long Zellerhaus would let him.

I had been in the same spot for an hour and a half. For the time I had invested I hadn't gotten much return. The traffic in nurses and maids had been zero for the past ten minutes, so I started the engine, turned around the drive and bounced out onto Connecticut. I stayed on it all the way to Lafayette Square and cut over to the parking garage. The afternoon still held a couple of useful hours and a few clients still had faith in me.

After Mrs. Bross's clucking had subsided, I went through the work on my desk and called Kellaway. He was out of his office but they paged him and he answered from an extension. I said, "Did you bounce Redpath around or just press his pants lightly?"

"Sort of a mixture," Kellaway drawled. "About what we'd hand you in similar circumstances. All he'd admit was a matinée with Peachy from time to time. Claimed he didn't have a key."

"Believe him?"

"For now. Oh, yes, your name was mentioned. Seems you kind of forgot to tell me about Redpath."

"He seemed like a nice guy."

His voice hardened. "Leave any character analysis to me. The District pays me for it. You held out on me and it makes me boil every time I think of it."

"You owe me a couple yourself, so cancel one and forget it."

Thoughtfully Kellaway said, "Redpath got kind of wild when he told about finding you and his wife in a ritzy luncheonette."

"I know," I sighed. "All filled with righteous indignation. He was laying Peachy but me having lunch with his wife is a capital offense."

"That all?" Kellaway leered.

"That's all you're likely to hear about. Did your research develop the fact that Peachy had or has a younger sister?"

"Cobweb stuff. One of the lieutenants and a policewoman talked to her this morning. She's got a shack down along the C. and O. Canal with about ten other crumby beatniks. Community living. Mattresses on the floor, lunatic paintings on the walls and a stench like a burning carpet."

"Guess what it comes from, Captain."

"We're Homicide, not Narcotics," he said stuffily.

"Yeah. Roxy's improved herself since this morning. She touched Quinby for a couple of hundred skins. At the going rate that ought to keep her gang in pot for quite a while. You figure our Senator's developing a fatherly interest in the hip chick?"

"Do you?"

"Hell no. He wants his *sotto voce* romance kept as hushed as possible. Paying off Roxy is one way to achieve it."

"Anything more?"

"Ask the Senator."

"Someone suggested that earlier. We called his office and were informed he was back in the hills taking the pulse beat of grass-roots opinion."

"Mixed metaphor. I'm pretty sure he was around here this afternoon. The bread didn't drop from heaven into Roxy's pretty little lap."

"Yeah? We might look into that further."

"The hell you say. Interrogate a United States Senator, string tie, putty nose and all?"

"It could happen," he said cautiously. "Of course we'd have to locate him first."

"And the search could go on until Congress convenes in January. Don't diagram it for me. Meanwhile, who's your main suspect?"

"Redpath will do for now."

"Not bad," I mused. "Circumstantially a natural. And not so close to the Ward millions you'd have much trouble dropping a hoop over him. From what I gathered at lunch today that might be the ideal solution. Save Alma the expense and embarrassment of a divorce."

"If we pull the trap it'll be for a better reason than that," he said evenly. "Any further contributions?"

"Nothing of value. Shall we keep in constant touch?"

"That'll be up to you. Kind of."

The line went dead and I swiveled around in my chair. Through the window I could see an Electra screaming down for a landing across the river. Faraway places with strange sounding names, available at the touch of a checkbook. You chased your tail around Washington and ended up in the cellar. A lousy place to live. A worse place to work. Kellaway could tell you that. A couple more years of grinding down his brains and sinew and he'd be on White House duty, maybe heading the guard detail at Blair House, watching the comings and goings of those who made world news. Sideline pasture for a good cop. It seemed as though something kinder could be arranged.

Mrs. Bross buzzed me and I picked up the phone. For the next ten minutes I chatted with a Maryland client about a capital-gains problem involving stock purchase and resale. He seemed satisfied with my suggestions and thanked me. I scrawled a reminder to bill him for consultation and began riffling through other matters.

After a while Mrs. Bross stuck in a freshly powdered nose and bade me good-by. I got up, stretched and went over to the window. Below me the evening rat-race was in full swing. The sidewalks were filled with office workers and in the street a traffic jam had developed between cars headed for Virginia and others bound north to Maryland. People chasing their tails all day long and ending up nowhere. That was where Roxy's crowd had the rest of us beat. They didn't fool around with reality. They just ignored it.

From my desk I pulled out a bottle of seven-year-old and clamped my teeth around the open end. It tasted like ten-penny nails but I got down a couple of ounces, coughed and capped the bottle. It hadn't been one of my better days.

Turning out the lights, I went out of the office.

No smirking bolos waited for me outside the door. No saps whistled through the air. Nobody braced me and rode me back inside for a menacing chat. The corridor was empty. I liked it that way.

On my way to the garage I eased into a saloon and straddled a stool. Farther along half a dozen bar buzzards were plucking the booze bush and studying their scratch sheets. The booths held couples and groups of office girls. The only gaiety in the place came in bottles. A lonely town. A town where you grew old and everyone grew old along with you. I ordered a double Gibson.

"Olive or onion?" the bartender asked.

I shrugged. "Just so long as the glass is edible."

He let it rattle by and got busy with his ice and bottles. From the end of the bar a woman was watching me. A woman in her mid-thirties with auburn hair, arched eyebrows and a cool glance. She smiled carelessly and lifted her glass. I caught the glint of a wedding band and looked away. A Navy wife, maybe, with a traveling husband, or maybe not even that much of an excuse. Lonely like the rest of us or on the prowl. Another night I might have taken the trouble to find out. Instead I kicked down my Gibson, laid some bread on the bar and slouched out.

In my apartment I shucked my coat and dialed Alma Ward's snuggery. The same maid with the same German accent answered me. Miss Ward had come in, changed and gone out. No, she had left no message. I thanked her, left my name, and hung up. Then I took a shower and drove out to a client's restaurant to eat up part of my credit. After that I idled back to my pad and turned in.

CHAPTER ELEVEN

It was ten o'clock in the morning and Artie Von Amond was in my office. He was saying, "Not much on Nagle, Steve. From Quinby's home state. Took a high-school commercial course and went to business college in Wilmington. About the time of Korea he was in the Coast Guard."

"A patriot."

"Yeah." He opened the collar of his tieless sport shirt, straightened his shapeless cuff and consulted his notes. "Got one of those colored discharges that means nothing—or something."

"In his case I'll settle for the latter."

"Nagle may also be about a fourth cousin of the Senator's. Through Nagle's mother's family."

"Nepotism? Heaven forbid."

Artie chuckled. "You know how it is up in Li'l Abner country. They get kinda careless of things like marriage certificates and birth registration documents."

"Not without reason. Is he a doper?"

"No record. That doesn't mean he doesn't do it discreet."

"He'd be the discreet type," I muttered.

"Nagle's been working for Quinby the last three years. Salary's close to fourteen grand. Not bad for answering the telephone and punching constituents' T.S. cards. With maybe a little pimping tossed in."

"We should have it so good."

He adjusted his notes, breathed heavily and said, "Quinby's finishing out his third term. You know where he comes from and all that so we'll skip it. He'll be sixty-five in a couple of months. Started out as a hillbilly J.P. and got a mail-order law degree while same was still possible. County judge, then a term as lieutenant-governor. A part term in the House. Quit to run for the Big Club and made it. Been having a running battle with the Governor over who's in charge of patronage. Wife's been in a private buggery for nine years."

"That's all Public Library stuff, Artie."

"More coming." He lighted a cigarette and grinned. "Ever hear of a heavy man named Babe Horton?"

"Not lately."

"There's a reason." He settled back in his chair and hooked a knee over the arm. "When I was still on the Force the Babe was a Baltimore peter gee responsible for kiting theft insurance rates around town. A few years back he knocked off the Sobel Fur Shop safe and skinned out with close to forty grand. Then he disappeared. For a while nobody could figure it and there was some talk he'd gone to Europe or South America. Then word got around he was serving time. Not in Maryland, though. Turned out that after the Sobel job he lit out for French Lick to sort of enjoy the loot, taking back roads, and drifted through a crossroads town one night. He was going slow enough to notice a country bank—old frame building and no lights. Well, temptation overcame him. Babe went through the window, a couple sticks of Dinah in his pocket and started stuffing the safe. Someone hollered at him and the Babe dived through the window. He didn't crawl far because by then there was a forty-four slug in his hip. Turned out the bank had been robbed a week before and the sheriff was sleeping there nights." Artie inhaled a long drag and let smoke drift across his knee. "In that part of the country they look on bank robbing as sort of a personal offense. The jury dealt the Babe fifteen years in state prison, and believe me, where he's been makes Leavenworth look like a Turkish harem."

"Fascinating," I said. "Only what's the Babe got to do with our parcel of characters?"

He gazed at me wisely. "More than you might think. When they frisked the Babe he had only half the Sobel loot on him. Where d'you suppose the other half had gone?"

"Salvation Army."

"Hell, Steve, think a little. The Babe was from Baltimore— Maury Renzo's town. Nothing could be proved, but Maury's usual take was an even split. The Babe's been in stir a long weary time. Under standing arrangements he's got a right to expect Maury to give him a hand. I don't mean bank his money at three per cent, either. I mean put in the fix. Babe's locked up in prison in a state where Quinby pulls plenty of rope. Now, by sheer coincidence, Quinby's petitioned the Governor for a pardon for the Babe. Nice, huh?"

"Sweet as buckwheat honey. I dig."

His eyebrows drew together. "Hey, you gone beat?"

"I had a close brush but no permanent effects. Not a bad piece of research, Artie. The dirt that never hits the headlines."

"Maybe so. On the other hand the pardon hasn't moved very far. There's this struggle between Quinby and the Governor to control the state machine and the Governor isn't doing Quinby any favors for free. There'll have to be something in it for him, too."

"Yeah. With Quinby, Renzo and the Governor biting it Babe's twenty grand would chew down to zero pretty fast."

"And maybe no pardon afterward."

"There'll be a pardon," I said. "Those guys have got a reputation to maintain. Otherwise confidence might be destroyed and the system would fall apart. Like labor and capital, they'll work it out. At someone else's expense."

"Little cynical today?"

"Possibly. Last night wasn't even Saturday night and it scored a knife killing, three muggings and a gang attack on a patrolman.

All in the streets of our city. Cynical could just be the word for my outlook."

He shook his head. "It'll be worse before it gets better. As if you didn't know."

"Yeah. Anything more on Quinby?"

"Not directly. He's got the name of being on the Zellerhaus payroll. No proof of that. As for Zellerhaus, he was sort of a quiz-kid lawyer; hooked into some government jobs, made the rounds and got himself known. Then he set himself up in the lobby racket. Influence-peddling. A wife somewhere in the background. He represents maybe five or six pressure groups."

"Including Maury Renzo."

"So they say."

"Take it from Bentley," I said.

"Okay. Larry gives a lot of parties, hits most of the race meets and burrows around Washington like a rat in Swiss cheese. He's seen with fancy women and respectable people, too. Has plenty of powerful friends."

"And some powerful enemies," I said. "At least one I know of. Alma Ward."

His eyes widened. I filled a pipe, lighted it and told him the story. Part of it he liked, other parts he didn't. When I finished he said, "Little out of your usual line, Steve."

"My usual line is being a C.P.A. and advising people on tax matters. If we're talking about my secret life I'd say it's about average."

He stubbed out his cigarette and unhooked his leg. "Want me to keep digging?"

"That's enough. I just wanted the basic facts."

"You've got them," he said and stood up. He folded his notes and pocketed them. "The papers say a suspect for the Bolac murder has been jailed."

"Jailed and released," I told him. "Part of a little plan."

"Not Kellaway's." He grinned.

"I may have given him the idea. The field's rich with candidates, Artie. Too rich. They need weeding out and that might take a little time. Meanwhile, no reason to make the killer feel insecure."

"None at all. You got some thoughts?"

"Some," I admitted. "The stumbler is the rape angle."

"That oughta ease it. You start out eliminating dames. Or in my time you did."

"Ever hear of transvestites?"

"Sure. But I never knew one." He leered evilly. I leered back and Artie went out. I buzzed for Mrs. Bross and she came in, shorthand notebook in hand.

"Call the office of Mr. Lawrence Zellerhaus and get me an appointment. If there's any question, put me on."

"Yes, sir."

I fumbled around, relighting my pipe and after a while she buzzed back. I picked up the phone and heard the Zellerhaus voice. Whipped cream this time. "Bentley? Nice of you to call. Sure, come over any time." He cleared his throat. "Alone, of course."

"Like Lindbergh."

"Fine," he said expansively. "I'll look forward to seeing you. About two, say."

I replaced the receiver. Let bygones be bygones, I thought bitterly. And I'll look forward to seeing *you,* you fat-faced son of a bitch. At the wrong end of a pistol barrel. Like you'd never had me slapped around. Like you hadn't planned to boot me in concrete and drop me in the river.

I could feel my face getting hot. I shook myself and rummaged through the pile of work on my desk. Selecting an easy case, I finished it in an hour and sent out for coffee.

When Mrs. Bross brought it in she said, "A lady would like to see you, Mr. Bentley." Her eyebrows arched. "I rather imagine you would like to see her."

"Did she have a name?" I asked, "or are we playing it extra cozy this month?"

"Miss Ward," she sniffed. "Miss Alma Ward. Shall I have her come in?"

I picked up the cardboard container. "Have her sit where she is. You know the rules. Coffee break is inviolate."

"Really, Mr. Bentley," she wheezed and whisked out.

Tilting back in my chair I sipped the coffee. As usual, someone had added sugar. Pulling the bottle from my drawer I added an ounce to cut it, sampled the mix and put the bottle away.

As I sipped I thought about Alma and relived yesterday's scene at the Colmenar. There had been a lot of implications there and I had probably not caught all of them. And Alma had been as talkative as an ice sculpture. Then, last night, she had stood me up. I wondered what her mood would be today. Whatever it was, it probably wouldn't improve with waiting.

When the little container was empty I crumpled it and lofted it into the waste basket. Then I buzzed twice.

Mrs. Bross opened my door and closed it behind Alma Ward. She was wearing silk shantung today, beige, with matching shoes and a white piqué hat. Walking directly toward me she halted at the edge of the desk and snapped, "Was making me wait really necessary?"

"You're a businesswoman. You understand how business is. The exigencies, the necessity to keep tight schedules."

Her nostrils flared. "I thought our relationship might have allowed for an occasional concession on your part."

"That's trading on sex," I said. "Never part of the bargain."

"If one was ever made." Her cheeks were flushed. High color accented her fine cheekbones, gave her lips a pouty nubile look. "I suppose this is your way of punishing me for last night."

"Possibly. I thought you'd want time to prepare a good excuse."

"After the casual way you left me yesterday? My invitation was clear and to the point. I gathered you couldn't have cared less."

"That was only superficial. Deep down inside my conscience was gnawing me."

"I'll bet," she said scornfully. "A practiced Lothario like you having conscience trouble?"

I grinned at her. "You have a way of saying the nicest things, gorgeous. Take a chair or come over here and curl up in my lap. Then make your excuses."

She swerved sideways and sat down in a chair. Glaring at me, she whipped a cigarette from her handbag. I watched her light it. Blowing smoke across the desk, she said, "Sometimes you display the manners of a stevedore. Other times not. Altogether you're impossible."

"Agreed," I said. "Now the preliminary fencing's behind us, why did you come here?"

Her eyes glinted. "Are you interested enough to listen?"

"Try me," I said soothingly.

"Very well." She crossed her legs and smoothed the line of her skirt. Absolutely fantastic legs. "I received a telephone call yesterday afternoon. It was a man's voice and it was disguised. They use a handkerchief, don't they?"

"They can," I said. "Not that it helps much."

"Well, this was an unfamiliar voice. The man made me a proposal."

"Indecent? It must happen often."

"What an obscene mind," she hissed. "No, it was no would-be lover. It was a man who said he could deliver the recording made in Peachy's apartment. The one featuring Zellerhaus and Senator Quinby." Leaning back, she inhaled smugly.

"Think of that," I said, sitting forward. My body had gone tense. "For what kind of a consideration?"

"Ten thousand dollars."

I licked my lips. "Sounds high. But that's just the first offer. He'll come down. After all, it's a restricted market."

"He could sell it to Zellerhaus or Quinby, couldn't he?"

"If he wanted to take larger chances. You've got money, you want the recording. It isn't likely your interest extends beyond that."

She shook her head. "It doesn't."

I laced my fingers and stared at her. "Just a straight commercial transaction. How is the switch to be made?"

"Are you so sure it hasn't taken place?"

"You couldn't resist telling me if it had."

Her face clouded. "Damn you. No, I don't have it yet. I expected to, but it's to happen later on."

"When?"

Her lips set. "Steve, don't think you can stop me. This is my business, not yours."

I felt my face grow hard. "What happened last night?"

She adjusted herself in the chair and avoided my gaze. "He told me to go to a drugstore across the District line."

"Where?"

"Silver Spring. I was to be there at seven and wait for contact to be made."

"Was it?"

"Yes. I sat at the counter drinking coffee until nearly eight. Then the pay phone rang and the manager answered it. The call was for me."

"The tryout," I muttered.

"It was the same voice. He said he was glad I had followed instructions and come alone. He said I would get another call today and further instructions. This time I'm to bring the money."

"How much?"

"We agreed on eight thousand."

"I see." I took a pipe from the rack, filled and lighted it slowly. When it was going well I looked at her again. Her face was eager and proud. A woman in a man's game, and winning as usual. I said, "Let's consider the facts, sweetheart. You got Peachy Bolac to make a clandestine recording for you. When you asked for delivery she held out for more cabbage. You went back to pay her and take delivery but she was passed out. Next scene: Peachy dead and the recorder gone. Along with the recording and Quinby's picture."

"We know all this," she said petulantly.

"Of course. Now to me the facts, as known, point to the strong likelihood of Peachy's having been killed in revenge for, or to get possession of, the recording. And several persons would have had that kind of motivation."

She nodded impatiently.

"Those persons are known to you as well as to me. Next, you get a mysterious phone call and go through the flimflam of a *subrosa* turnover. All running true to form and practice. Doesn't it occur to you that you might be running some danger?"

"I've thought of it," she admitted.

"But you haven't told any of this to the police?"

"Of course not. Why should I? It's my money, isn't it? And you know what I want the recording for."

"Ah, yes. *Washington Scene*. Sunday afternoons at three. A confrontation in the classic tradition. That defines and limits your interest."

Her face had grown cautious. The ash was long on her cigarette but she had forgotten it. I said, "Has it never occurred to you that the man you're dealing with is probably the man who raped and murdered Peachy Bolac?"

"Yes," she said uneasily.

"And that this is the first direct contact anyone has had with the murderer since the crime? And that if this were played right the police probably could bag him?"

"I've thought of all that," she said in a remote voice. "The difference is the man isn't dealing with the police. He's dealing with me. Once I have the recording I don't care what happens to him. Until then, the only important thing to me is getting it into my possession."

"If you'd tell the police they'd probably co-operate with you."

"It's a risk that doesn't appeal to me. Why should I?"

"Because that man killed Peachy Bolac in a slow and horrible way."

She stood up, flushing. "I don't want any lectures on my civic responsibilities. I came here because I thought you might want to help me—possibly eliminate some of the danger you keep mentioning. As for any feeling I have about that little Bolac whore, I could put it all in a thimble and still have room for my finger."

My throat was dry. I stared at her. "She was a human being," I grated. "Her death deserves to be avenged. Compared to that your interest shows up as a pretty tawdry article. Ever since we met I've been wondering how Redpath could have given you up. Now it comes to me. He wanted a human being for a wife, someone with a heart and normal emotions. And you couldn't qualify."

Her voice was brittle as sheet ice. "You're sentimental," she said. "That's why you'll always be where you are—a cheap little man in a cheap little business. My father would never—"

"Your father's ethics were well known," I snarled. "Too bad you didn't inherit something from your mother's side. Once I saw two dogs playing at the side of the road. A truck ran down one and killed it. Its friend went over to it. I expected it to lick the dead one's muzzle or begin whining." I shook my head. "Nothing of the kind. It nosed the dead friend for a moment and then lifted its leg on it. That's the animal kingdom; it's what we expect of animals. Of humans we expect a little more. Even hoodlums send flowers to each other's funerals."

Her face had twisted, her teeth were bared. Whirling, she strode out and the door slammed shut.

I was shaking. The outer door closed behind her and by then I had the bottle in my hand. My throat felt as if I had been swallowing old razor blades. The liquor hit it and stung. All the way down. I wiped my lips and put the bottle away. Compared to Alma Ward, Roxy Bolac was another Florence Nightingale.

My pipe had gone out. I shook a cigarette from the pack and lighted it and my hand was still trembling. It wouldn't do any good to tell it to Kellaway. He'd need Alma's co-operation to bring anything off.

But between now and Alma's final phoned instructions I might be able to figure something out.

CHAPTER TWELVE

It was an old brownstone house on the west side of Jackson Place, facing Lafayette Square. The trees in the park were heavy with summer leaves and gray squirrels chased across the lawn. On a bench two elderly tourists shared a snack and tossed crumbs to pigeons that fluttered down from the statue of General Von Steuben. On a shady bench sat an old man in a Panama hat, staring at nothing. His eyes were pouched with age and his face was grizzled. From his posture he could have been an old soldier, one of the heroes of Verdun. Now left with only the memory of ancient battles and fading rollcalls of dead comrades. In fair weather he would be there every day, at the same appointed time. In winter he would sit in his room and stare out at the falling snow. Just waiting.

As I climbed the staircase I saw a polished brass plate beside the door. Engraved in large script was the name: *Lawrence Zellerhaus Attorney-at-Law*. Attorney-outside-the-law, I thought, and leaned on the button.

The door opened and I stepped up into an air-conditioned reception hallway. Behind me the door closed and street sounds faded. From the thick carpeting to the colored window glass at the far end the whole place whispered conservatism and quiet discretion. The lady who had opened the door was on the far side of sixty, with a lace-collared dress and a face as dry as a split cod. In a voice equally dry she said, "Mr. Bentley? Mr. Zellerhaus will see you now." Turning, she walked toward a double oak door and I was glad to see that she wore low-heeled sensible shoes. Spike heels would have caught in the rug's thick nap.

Opening one side of the door, she stood aside. I passed through and saw a room decorated in the same heavily Victorian style as the dowager Mrs. Ward's. The walls were covered with beige tapestry figured with a woven gold design. There were Currier & Ives prints on the walls, framed in antique gilt. An ancient bookcase held a convincing collection of law books. The desk was dark massive oak, illuminated by a wired hurricane lamp. Everything about the place was sincere. All except the modern touch of a corner cellarette. Behind its polished panels there would be a cube freezer and enough bottle space to supply a lodge meeting.

The man who stood behind the desk was no stranger to me. I had seen him once before. Also behind a desk. He looked as though he had divided the morning among the Turkish bath, the club barber and the manicurist. He was wearing a navy-blue suit of Italian silk that must have cost at least two hundred and fifty dollars. His white poplin shirt had a sheen like new-fallen snow and his dark tie was figured with Royal Coachman flies. Very cool and very plausible.

His back was to the window light but I could see something flicker across his face. He started to offer his hand, decided against it and jammed it into his coat pocket. I found a chair and sat down. That left him still standing. He didn't like it. He had decided in advance to dominate the scene but the details weren't quite working out. Abruptly he cleared his throat and sat down. There was no bluster in his voice when he spoke. "I appreciate you coming over like this. Actually I should have gotten in touch with you before."

"You're damn right you should have."

It ruffled him. He frowned slightly and picked up a slip of paper and worried one thumbnail with it. "I think we can work this out so there'll be no hard feelings."

"How?" I asked. "Just what would your idea be?"

He cleared his throat and lifted what his fingers held. "I have here a check for a thousand dollars, Mr. Bentley."

I got up and walked over to the desk. I took the check from his hand and glanced at it. "So that's my price," I murmured. "I'm supposed to take, this, walk out of here and forget the beating your gorilla gave me the other night. Is that the picture?"

He looked up and his lips twitched but no sound came.

Lowering my hands, I let the check slide onto the desk. "It's not enough," I rasped, "and if it were more and I took it I'd be letting you off too easy. You might even think I was really a patsy and get ingenious again. So take your check, Mr. Zellerhaus. I'll take this."

My left hand shot across the desk and grabbed his tie. I jerked up and back. Hard. His hands scrabbled on the desk top, papers were sliding everywhere. His face was as white as his shirt. Strangled sounds came from his throat. My right hand drew back and slapped his cheeks. Very precisely and very hard. The backhand return caught the corner of his mouth and a drop of blood fell onto the desk. Then I heaved him back into his chair. His hands clawed to loosen the noose of his tie and his mouth made whimpering sounds. His face was ghastly white. All except for the red spots on his cheekbones and the ooze of blood on his mouth. I leaned forward and snarled, "If you think that's excessive, send Baldy around again. After that you could buy him a set of gold teeth. If he was still warm enough to care."

His eyes were wild with fear. He cringed into the burrow of his chair and stared at me. I said, "There's something for sale, Zellerhaus. Something new on the market. Yesterday it was offered for the first time. The asking price is ten thousand dollars."

"Wha... what is it?" he burbled.

"You're the wizard with built-in radar," I sneered. "Figure it out. It's what got Peachy Bolac killed. It's the recording she made of you and Quinby that afternoon not so long ago. Made public it's enough to put you and Quinby on the rock pile until they run out of rocks. The killer's got it, Zellerhaus. He wants ten thousand skins. If I were you I'd make a deal before the price goes up. Or before it falls into unfriendly hands."

His face twitched. The comfortable layer of fat had shrunken away, leaving too much skin. For what was left the eyes were too large, the lips too thick. "Christ," he gasped, "I wouldn't know how to ... Bentley, you got to help me!"

"Stop the clowning," I grated. "Me help *you?* Just telling you has made my day complete. There's a little time left, Zellerhaus. Not much, but you just might make it."

Turning, I strode back across the room of a house that had been built for finer things, jerked open the door and went down the quiet hallway. The receptionist darted out of her chair but I reached the door first and slammed it shut. Squaring my shoulders, I went down the stone steps and crossed into the park.

The tourist couple had eaten and left. All that remained was a brown bag and some wax paper stirring in the gentle breeze. Pulling out a cigarette, I lighted it and slowed my pace. The old man was still sitting in the shade, still staring at nothing. On the third finger of his left hand was a heavy gold ring worn almost entirely smooth. The center mounted a cracked red stone. A Military Academy class ring. Once you've seen them you never forget. When I was beside the old gentleman I stopped and said, "Good afternoon, General. A good day to be alive, sir."

He looked up and I saw his eyes glint. Entirely composed he said, "Colonel. Though I thank you for the tombstone promotion."

"There's not so much difference," I said and looked around. "I kind of like a place where squirrels can run and children can play. In the midst of a big city like this."

"I enjoy it, too, sir," he said in an even voice. "It is fortunate that I do, so little being left to occupy my time."

"But you have proud memories."

He nodded slowly. "Some proud, others painful. I remain a misfit in a world that has turned its attention to other things. Sometimes I think of myself as driftwood cast aside by a swift unmanageable current. Just how did you know I was a soldier, sir?"

"The shoulders," I said. "After plebe year they lock that way. That and the straight spine."

He smiled. It was a distant smile, as though pleasant memories had been touched. Then it was gone. "We called it military bearing," he mused. "Or perhaps you know. Tell me, where did you serve?"

"Korea," I said, "and I wish you hadn't asked."

"I understand. The war we lost. Of it a famous officer said that it happened in the wrong place at the wrong time. I happen to disagree. If our concept of defense is to fight only wars of our own choosing then we have no defense at all. None at all. There was, however, one important thing lacking in your war, sir. Perhaps you know what it was."

I said nothing, waiting for him to say it.

His eyes left me and he stared straight ahead. "The will to win. Always an essential ingredient."

I nodded.

Turning, he gazed through the trees at the White House shining distantly in the afternoon sun. "Who occupies that residence is not important, sir. My years have taught me that. What is important is the marrow of our country." He looked back at me. "Forgive me if I suggest that we have grown soft with comfort; indifferent to others from serving ourselves. I suggest that today there are ideals more worthy of our efforts. More honorable."

"Honor," I said moodily. "Almost a forgotten word."

"Never believe that," he said sharply. "If I did I should greet death with gratitude." Then his voice softened and I thought I saw his eyes mist over. "Thank you for stopping, sir. I enjoyed our encounter. Perhaps you'll stop another day."

"I will, sir," I said gently and moved on.

Overhead a flicker was drumming industriously on the branch of an old elm. Pigeons clustered over the statue of

Lafayette. Two squirrels played hide-and-seek around the trunk of a willow. Summer afternoon in Lafayette Square. But by night a promenade for nolas and thrush-voiced perverts. The underground lavatories had been the center once, but the Vice Squad had managed to get them closed, forcing the angelinas above into the shadowed park.

At Madison Place I waited for the signal to change and crossed. Walking one block south I went into a pharmacy and slid into the phone booth. A thin dime got me Artie Von Amond on the horn.

"Things have picked up a little," I said. "I just put Zellerhaus on the send. I want two men, one watching his place from a park bench, the other in a car parked along Jackson Place. I want to know where Zellerhaus goes the rest of the day, who he sees. Can do?"

"Can do," Artie said grudgingly. "Is he tipped to a tail?"

"He's got bigger worries. I want hourly reports, if possible."

"It's remotely possible," Artie said. "I wish just once you could give me maybe an hour's notice when you want a job like this."

"It's a restless life," I observed. "I can barely keep up with it myself."

"You sticking to your office?"

"There and elsewhere. I'll keep track of myself, you worry about Zellerhaus."

The phone clicked down and I pushed out of the booth.

At the souvenir counter two flustered teachers were trying to buy and distribute pennants and Confederate hats to twenty sixth-graders. One of the teachers carried a flag with the legend: *Hawkins Junior High. Hawkins, Kansas.* Up from the alfalfa country for a gape at the Nation's Capital. The clamor and shouting got louder but the clerks were used to it. They did their business as coolly as supply sergeants but it was a lot tougher on the teachers. Washington was a national shrine in the same way as the bronze Buddha at Kamakura. Once in his lifetime every native was expected to view it. And usually did.

The street again. A hot sunny block to my office, the greased whir of the elevator and corridor coolness. As I went inside I pulled off my coat and loosened my tie. Mrs. Bross was tinkling her specialized music on the Burroughs and my blinds were closed. Opening them, I turned back to the desk and saw a phone call notation: *Pls call Mr. Ray Stroud.*

Reaching for the phone, I sank into the chair and began dialing. When Stroud answered I identified myself and heard him say, "Captain Kellaway tol' me you was willin' to stand my bond, Mistah Bentley. I'm sure mighty grateful."

"Forget it."

"No, suh. I surely won't." He coughed and then he said, "I went up to Mis' Bolac's apartment fo' a look around. Being's it's next to you I thought you'd want to know."

"Know what, Ray?"

"Why, someone got in there an' tore the place apart. Must of been lookin' for somethin'. Manager's sure mad, too. Cushions ripped and tore, mattresses all pulled apart, drawers turned upside down. Somethin' crazy."

"Have the police been notified?"

"Not by me, no suh. Not after the trouble I already had. I'm jus' callin' you. Tha's all."

"You call Captain Kellaway, too. He won't blame you. In fact he'll appreciate the information."

"You sure about that, suh?"

"I'm sure," I said. "Thanks, Ray."

I hung up and stared at my desk blotter. Only the expected, after all. Not much there. It wouldn't have been the killer making the search—he'd got his before and gone. That made it one of the other interested parties: Redpath or Quinby and Company. Most likely Baldy had done the job. Or even Nagle. And it was possible that Roxy Bolac had a key and had used it to look around on her own. Everyone looking for something that was no longer there; something that was being peddled by the murderer. Today.

Pulling out my bottle, I sucked on it a while and thought things over. Then I capped it and put it away. Pulling on my coat, I straightened my tie and went out. To Mrs. Bross I said, "I doubt I'll be back today, though I may call in from time to time. If Mr. Von Amond calls, just take the message."

"Yes, sir. Will you be in tomorrow?"

"God willing," I said and left.

Ransoming the Olds I took Pennsylvania to Washington Circle and cut up into Georgetown. Shutters were closed against the afternoon's stagnant heat and a lone trolley clanged hollowly up Wisconsin. I turned west on P Street and north on 35th, then onto Volta Place.

There wasn't a lot of spare curb space but I managed to park on the north side of the street less than a block from Alma Ward's house. Trees blocked the door from view but I could see her Riley parked outside. I was gambling that Alma was inside waiting for the killer's call but the parked Riley wasn't conclusive evidence. She could be downtown in her office, business as usual, and planning to taxi to the rendezvous.

It was now three o'clock, the sun was high overhead and my Olds was only partly shaded. Rolling down the windows, I loosened my tie, lighted a cigarette and tried to make myself comfortable. With luck Artie's two men were in place, covering Zellerhaus. With more luck I would see Alma drive off to meet the killer. Turning on the radio I found a record program, slouched behind the wheel and closed my eyes.

Bees droned through a nearby rose bush. Overhead birds cheeped and twittered. A plane whistled through the sky, sliding down toward National Airport. The distant sounds of traffic blurred in the humid air. Groggily, I butted my cigarette and closed my eyes again.

The sound of a car engine woke me. I grabbed the wheel and relaxed. It was the Riley, all right. No need to poke my head up and rubberneck. It glided past me as quietly as an electric submarine and when it slowed at the corner I started the Olds and looked around.

She was turning north on 35th, a one-way street.

The Olds was faced wrong, but I could still get behind her. I tore away from the curb and turned north on 33rd, cutting back over on Reservoir Road. When I swerved onto 35th the Riley was less than two blocks ahead of me, moving at an easy pace.

Snapping off the radio, I settled back against the seat and idled along after the maroon Riley.

CHAPTER THIRTEEN

At R Street she turned right, skimmed past Oak Hill cemetery and on over to Q. Then around Sheridan Circle and onto 22nd Street, holding until it merged northbound with Connecticut. It seemed like a long way around to get there from Volta Place, but maybe Alma was killing time. Closing our distance, I followed her another five blocks. Then, just south of Taft Bridge, she turned left onto a graveled terrace, slowed to a crawl, found a space and parked.

I knew the spot. I had been there only yesterday. It was where I had exchanged snarls with Roxy Bolac: the apartment house of Senator Quinby.

Alma got out of the Riley and crossed quickly into the entrance. I turned onto Ashmead Place and braked the Olds. The drive had done away with my Volta Place drowsiness, and seeing Alma enter the building quickened my blood. I looked at my watch, filched a cigarette from the pack and lighted it. If she had gone there for the turnover it shouldn't take long—just long enough for the killer to count his money and—and what? Kill Alma, too?

Bending over, I opened the glove compartment and extracted a bundle of greasy flannel. Looking around, I laid it on the seat, unwrapped it and lifted out my Walther P-38. I slid a shell into the chamber and dropped it in my coat pocket. Then I shoved the flannel wrapper back into the glove compartment.

The Olds was facing down a gentle grade. By half turning I could look up and across Connecticut and see the apartment entrance. The Riley was partly hidden by a high stand of bushes, but if and when Alma pulled away I would notice it. So far things were pretty well rigged. What happened from now on was up to her—and the killer.

The late afternoon traffic was sparse and quiet. Cars droned on and off Taft Bridge and over on the far side of the canyon the Shoreham gleamed in the slanting sunlight. Sweat slid along my face. I wiped with my coatsleeves and felt a little cooler. About a millionth of a degree. My cigarette was soggy. I tossed it out of the window and lighted another. Just then someone came out of the apartment. A woman, but not Alma. Someone older and less smartly dressed. She came as far as the curb and began making tentative gestures with her handbag. Finally a cab stopped and whisked her away. Two men went into the apartment building. I couldn't see their faces but by their backs they were strangers.

I checked my watch. Ten minutes had gone by. Sweat from my lip had sogged another cigarette. Tossing it away, I gave up.

The transaction was taking a little longer than I had figured. I decided to wait another five. I sat there staring around at the apartment entrance, my neck and shoulder muscles cramped and groaning. The minutes trudged by slower than chain-gang convicts.

Finally I turned around, mopped my face again and opened the door. As I slid out the Walther bumped the panel with a sound like a sledgehammer. I covered it inside my pocket with my right hand to keep my coat from swaying. Then I walked up to the curb, waited for two cars to pass, and crossed the street.

The building had six stories and a recessed front. Everything about it was old, massive and well cared for. Probably a co-operative with units starting at thirty thousand, when one was available. And the waiting list would read like the roster of the Cosmos Club.

A lobby floor of polished slate and thick oriental carpets, leaded-glass windows and spear-hung tapestries on the stone support columns. No beady-eyed bellhops and no shopworn boosters in the lobby. Instead, heavy oak chairs and a reading table big enough for King Arthur and two dozen knights. A conservative reception counter with a businesslike young man behind it doing accounts. He didn't look up as I crossed the lobby and I didn't shout at him.

Two elevators against the far wall. I pressed a button and a door slid silently open. No uniformed operator to study my face and wonder about the bulge in my pocket. I nudged the floor button and the door slid shut. The elevator hummed upward and a little ceiling fan made a feeble attempt to stir the hot air. I mopped my face again, but this time the perspiration was cold. Colder than a mountain brook. In my hand the pistol was cold, too; my fingers frozen.

The elevator whirred to a gentle stop and the doors slid open. I got out.

The hall carpet was dark brown and deeper than quicksand. Series numbers and an arrow pointed to where the Senator's apartment would be. Farther down the corridor and around the bend. I followed.

As I walked I studied the walls, the solid oak doors. The place would be soundproof to anything short of an infantry regiment reunion. A leaded window cast a slanting beam of light across the hall. Beyond it I saw the Senator's door.

It was oak like all the rest and numbered in wrought iron. Also like all the others. Only one thing distinguished it. The door was slightly open.

Halting before it, I looked up and down the hall, listened for a moment, and then peered in.

Through the crack I could make out furniture, a couple of lamps and part of a sofa. Very dimly. On the far side of the room a window shade had been partly raised. My thumb slid off the safety and I kneed the door inward. "Alma," I called.

The word didn't echo. It dropped like a bag of dust. I took two steps into the dimness and closed the door behind me. Then a smell hit my nostrils and crackled. It was only a faint scent, bitter and sour, but it snapped my head around as if it had been ammonia. The acrid smell was gunpowder. Smokeless powder and burned. Tendrils of it hung in the still air. I brushed them aside and moved forward. My vision was getting better now, my eyes were accommodating to the dimness. Along the back of my neck the hairs had prickled upright. I took another step forward.

I was in the living room, a nearly dark dining room to my left. To the right another dim room, a study. Ahead of me was the sofa and an end table with a reading lamp. I leaned over and turned it on.

The scent of smokeless seemed stronger on my right. Gun in hand I moved toward the study. Then, at the doorway I stopped. From where I stood I could see a woman's shoe. A white shoe, turned sideways. Alma had worn white shoes. Sucking in a deep breath I crossed through the open doorway and saw her.

She was lying on the floor, eyes closed, her right foot under the left ankle. Her hands were curled naturally and her lips were partly open. Her bosom moved in shallow lifts and her face was as white as tallow. Stooping down I took her wrist and felt the pulse. It was there all right, slow and even, but otherwise normal. Her hair lay neatly in place. No blood or facial bruises. Just a hell of a place to pass out.

Getting up slowly, I looked around the study. Books in built-in bookcases. An antique Florentine desk with papers on it, a chaise longue, and a leather easy chair. What it held made my muscles jerk.

In it sat a man. Hands gripped the arms of the chair as though he were trying to pull himself out of it. Whatever had made him decide to rise was no longer important. He would never finish the thought, complete the action. He was as dead as mortal man can be. Turning quickly, I went to the window and lifted one of the shades. Light glinted from the dead man's bared teeth. From a gold tooth set in his lower jaw. His head was nearly bald and even in life his face had been ugly. Above the left eye and neatly centering his forehead was a small dark hole. The compression had bulged out both eyes, especially the left one. The fixed snarl and the popped staring eyes were on a par with any waxworks horror you ever saw. I made my way over to him and knelt to look for a gun. My hands searched under the chair and found nothing. No gun. But not really a surprise.

As I stood up I pocketed my Walther and picked up Baldy's left arm. It was still movable, but rigor was setting in. I replaced his arm and glanced back at Alma. Then I turned back and leaned over the dead body. The angle had shown me something I hadn't seen at first. Something black and shiny, wedged between his right hip and the side of the chair. It could have been gunmetal or it could have been polished ebony. I flicked on my lighter and lowered it. Then I flicked it off and got out a handkerchief.

Carefully I pulled the object out. It was an oblong case of heavy black plastic, about eight by four inches, and nearly two inches thick. It weighed close to two pounds. On one end was a metal trademark bearing an Italian name. I knew the brand. The other end had a woven handstrap. An inconspicuous little item looking not unlike a small transistor radio. There would be transistors inside it and miniature batteries and tiny magnets and a spool of magnetic tape. A tape recorder.

Carrying it over to the window, I set it on the sill and opened the top panel. The empty take-up spool was there and nothing more. Where the supply reel should have been there was only a round vacant recess.

A sound made me turn. Alma sighing. Her arms had moved. Leaving the recorder, I went over to her and lifted her head. Just then she opened her eyes.

Terror shadowed her face suddenly and her body snapped taut. Her throat made a small scream and then she sat upright. One hand went to her head, her face turned and then she looked back at me. Blankly.

I said, "Don't ask where you are, baby. You're here and nothing's changed. The only thing that's been added is me. If you don't want to see a corpse, don't look around. And don't scream. Baldy's done his last evil deed. He's as harmless as a statue."

Shakily she said, "I … I must have fainted."

"That or a professional imitation." Lowering a hand, I helped her up.

She stood swaying for a moment, one hand plucking her dress at her hips, and I thought she might faint again. Instead her chin straightened and she breathed deeply. "God," she whispered, "it was horrible. Just dreadful, Steve. You can't imagine."

"I'll struggle with it. We're in the apartment of Senator Tom Quinby, hardly a friend of yours. The dead thing in the chair used to work for Larry Zellerhaus. You came here to buy a reel of tape from a killer. What happened, then?"

"No," she said groggily. "I … I didn't come here for that."

"Care to confide in me? Bentley, the shopworn Samaritan?"

Turning, she said leadenly, "Don't, Steve … not now. I guess I'm a little out of my element." Bending over, she picked up her handbag. I took it from her, opened it, stared inside and gave it back.

"What was that for?" she said hostilely.

"Checking up. There was a chance you were lying. And more than just a chance. No money with you. Not eight thousand dollars, anyway. No tape spool either. And no gun. So far no lies. You came here, why?"

Her lips set. Evenly she said, "I came here to talk to Senator Quinby."

"On what subject?"

"To ask him to appear on *Washington Scene* two weeks from now. Any objections?"

Turning, I surveyed the room. Then I looked back at her. "No Senators here," I said. "Not even a freshman Representative. Just us chickens. You said you made an appointment with Quinby?"

"I said nothing of the kind," she snapped. "His office says he's out of town. I didn't believe it. I decided the only way to get him would be to come here. That way he couldn't refuse to appear."

"Why not?"

"I would have told him I would publicize the fact of his refusal."

"And that would have made him accept?"

Patiently she said, "Quinby has no reason to fear me. He doesn't know I have ... that I'll have the tape recording." Her shoulders straightened and she said, "I don't know why it's important, but that's the truth, darling. I swear it."

"Well," I said, "it's kind of nice to have someone think it's important you believe her. Now, how'd you get in?"

"The door was open." She glanced over my shoulder. "Steve! It's closed now!"

"I closed it, honey. I like to do my trespassing in private."

She smiled bleakly. "God, I'm glad you came. If I'd awakened and had to stare at that body again I think my heart would have stopped."

"You came in, looked around and saw nobody but the corpse?"

She nodded. "What do we do now?"

"That depends." I went over to the window, masked my hand with the handkerchief and brought back the tape recorder. Her eyes widened and she reached for it. I pulled it back, away from her hand.

"It's mine," she said in a brittle voice. "Give it to me."

"Not just yet. The police may want it as evidence." I pointed at the empty spool recess. "It doesn't have what you want, anyway, and it might be helpful to the police. Fingerprints, you know. Stodgy little technical details. This would be the one you gave Peachy to use?"

She nodded slowly, eyes narrowing.

"Fine. We'll just put it back where I found it."

I walked to the far end of the study and pushed the recorder down beside Baldy's right hip. Then I pocketed my handkerchief and went back to her. "It can't be traced to you, so don't fret. Anyway, what's a couple hundred bucks to you?"

Her eyes had gone hard. "I wonder," she said, thoughtfully. "I wonder if the dead man was the man who talked to me."

"The probability's high," I said. "What's left of the day should prove it one way or the other. You said you were going to get the recording later."

She nodded.

"Where and under what circumstances?"

"I don't know yet. The final message hasn't come."

I glanced at Baldy. The lips seemed to have drawn back even further. I wondered if he had really been born a woman. "Maybe it won't, sugar. But supposing it does—are you ready to co-operate with the police?"

She laughed hollowly. "After this? I may frighten easily but it doesn't last long. The answer to your question is no."

"You worry me," I told her. "You're a hard-hearted Hannah if I ever knew one, and you're smart enough that you ought to be scared stiff. If the call doesn't come that means you were probably dealing with Baldy all along. If it does—it means the caller not only throttled Peachy Bolac but shot Baldy as well. Your intention is to deal with a two-time killer all by yourself?"

"Precisely."

"Anything that happened, you'd have coming to you."

"I know that."

"Hell," I said, "you don't need old Launcelot Bentley. You don't need anyone at all. You're sort of like Sydney Carton ascending the scaffold, smug about the whole damn thing. You're begging to have your pretty little neck wrung."

One hand touched my lapel. "Please, Steve…"

"What time's the next contact with the killer?"

"Eight," she said, then bit her lip. "I didn't mean to tell you that. Now you'll try to follow me again."

"Suppose I just let you go to hell your own self-possessed way?"

"That might be the best solution."

"Diamond-hard, eh? Be off with you."

Her eyes flickered wide. "What are you going to do?"

"Keep our corpse company. Maybe he always wanted a wake."

She bent forward slightly and her lips brushed the side of my cheek. "Brute," she whispered. "Did you really expect to find a gun in my bag?"

"There was more than a remote possibility."

Moving back, she studied my face. "You thought I might have killed him and staged the rest?"

"You're capable of it. You've got the intelligence and the self-composure."

"But why? Why would I do a thing like that?"

"For your own devious ends, I suppose. And God knows what they might be. We could go into that another time—under less pressing circumstances."

She glanced at the corpse, her face paled, she turned and strode out of the study. When the door clicked shut behind her I went over to the window and pulled down the shade. The need for light was past. I didn't need to look at Baldy's forehead again to estimate the size of the slug that had torn through his skull. It would be somewhere between a .32 and a .38, or possibly a medium foreign caliber. It would be lodged inside the cranium or in the back of the chair. An easy find, and priceless evidence for the police.

Lighting a cigarette, I strolled into the living room and draped myself across the sofa. I gave her five minutes' start and then I got up and went out of the door and polished the knob. Leaving the door ajar, as I had found it, I rode the elevator down to the quiet lobby and went outside.

Traffic was heavier now, the northbound push to Maryland had begun and I waited for a stoplight before I crossed. When I was behind the wheel I got out the Walther, snapped on the safety and bundled it up in its flannel wrapper. Then I stowed it in the glove compartment, turned the Olds around and drove across the bridge.

At the first pharmacy I stopped and went into a phone booth. Dialing police headquarters, I barked an address at the desk sergeant and said, "Fifth floor, apartment twenty-two. Make all the noise you want; the stiff in the chair won't care."

"Hold it," he snapped, "who's this calling?"

"Peter Pan."

"P-A-N?" he queried.

"Step to the head of the class."

"What were you doing there, Mr. Pan?"

"Looking for my shadow."

"Your *what?*"

"My shadow," I drawled. "Thought I lost it there the other night. A big dog barked and I jumped out of it. But maybe it was another place." By then the receiver was crackling. I hung it up and stepped out of the booth. So much for Mr. Baldy. I allowed myself a slight shiver and got back into the car.

By now Artie might have something to report. I pulled away from the curb and joined the northbound lane. I needed a drink and a telephone. My apartment had both. I steered for it.

CHAPTER FOURTEEN

Finding Baldy dead changed things. Finding the recorder with him—but empty—changed them even more. If Baldy had been negotiating with Alma Ward for the tape recording, then he had in all probability also raped and murdered Peachy Bolac. He was dead now, the recorder beside him and minus the essential ingredient. If Baldy had ever had the little tape spool, it was missing now and very likely in the possession of a third party.

Or Baldy never had the tape recording at all. It was natural to associate the empty recorder with the missing spool, but not conclusive. If Baldy had ransacked Peachy's apartment last night he could have found the recorder there. Then Baldy could have made a rendezvous with the killer at Quinby's apartment in an effort to outbid Alma Ward, or Baldy could have thought a gun in the hand was more persuasive than eight grand in someone else's wallet. But all he had got out of the enterprise was a bullet in his skull. Leaving the whereabouts of the tape recording a continuing mystery.

It wasn't impossible that Alma had gone to the apartment, shot Baldy and extracted the spool from the recorder. She had been there a good fifteen minutes, plenty of time to take care of all the details, slip the gun in her girdle and drop the little spool in her bra. And there had been time enough to fake the fainting bit when she heard me open the door. About five seconds were all she would have needed. If it had happened that way.

The hard facts were few and sifted down to Baldy's death and the appearance of the emptied tape recorder. Someone had the gun that killed Baldy and very probably the tape recording as well. The rest was speculation.

I trooped up to the desk and asked for mail and messages. The clerk handed me a sheaf of direct mail advertisements and bills along with a couple of phone call memo forms. A bill from the Yacht Club for buoy rental for my ketch. A gas bill from Esso for the Olds. I pocketed them and got into the elevator. On the way up I read and discarded a summer sale notice from Saltz Brothers, an ad from a record club, a sale flyer offering window screens at half off, and a chance to buy a building lot cheap out in Lone Oak, Maryland. The phone call memos I kept.

Unlocking my door I went inside, broke out some ice cubes and constructed a medium-sized drink. One of the yellow forms stated that Mr. Von Amond had telephoned and wanted me to call back urgently. The other held Kellaway's name and a checked box indicated he would call again later. Fair enough.

Artie's voice was doleful. "Nothing happened, Steve. Either the boys got in position too late or Zellerhaus never left his office."

"They still there?"

"Sure. I wanted you to know, though. Night rates start at six. How much more coverage you want?"

"Six will do," I said. "After that I might take over myself."

"You're home now?"

"Yeah," I said, gazing around the empty room. "If you can call it home."

"Feeling a little morose?"

"Guess so. Thanks, Artie." I hung up and went over to the hi-fi cabinet and laid on a reel of Ella. Haunting, poignant music for the mood I was in. I listened to it and finished my drink. Then I pulled out the classified phone book and checked the electronic equipment section. The firm that sold the Italian tape recorders had an outlet near Chevy Chase Circle. I dialed the number and learned that the store was open another hour. Then I jotted down the address and pulled off my coat.

From the closet shelf I took down my shoulder holster and strapped it on. Empty, because the Walther was still in my glove compartment. While I was getting into my coat again the telephone rang.

It was Kellaway and he sounded crosser than usual. "Where you been all afternoon, Steve?"

"Here and there."

"Your travels didn't happen to include a layover on upper Connecticut, did they?"

"Precisely where?"

His voice hardened. "An apartment building near Taft Bridge—and a drugstore on the far side."

"Maybe I'm dull today—I don't get it."

"The hell you don't," he said savagely. "The Peter Pan touch makes it you. So does the description the pharmacist gave of the guy who called in. God dammit, I want the facts. Who killed Sammy Herod, and why?"

"That sounds like what you so frequently and charmingly refer to as police business—privileged information. Sammy Herod, you say? Never heard of him. Where would he be from— Bethlehem, Pa.?"

His voice got ugly. "As if you didn't know. Dead in Quinby's apartment. Bad news?"

"I can stand it. I never knew him. So long as you're publicity-minded I trust you'll give the papers the full facts, Captain. The Senator's just another citizen, after all. No reason to spare him the nasty publicity. Did you find the murder gun?"

"I didn't say a gun had killed him, so that clinches it. How'd you like to sweat out a few hours in the lineup?"

"Right now I'm a little short of time, Captain."

"Yeah? You might be startled if you knew how little that impresses me. Once the pharmacist picks you out of the lineup you'll have more than a little explaining to do."

"Captain," I said fervently, "if I had the least bitty piece of information I thought might help you I'd have told you by now."

"You tell me everything you know and *I'll* decide what might be helpful. C'mon, dammit, we're wasting time."

"Sorry," I said thoughtfully. "But if you really push me I'll have an alibi for all afternoon. A lady was involved."

Wrathfully he snarled, "A *lady* was involved, was she? Pray tell me her name—if it wouldn't violate any confidences."

"I'm afraid it would. It happens she's married, Captain, and you know how tricky a thing like that can be."

His voice was cold and level. "All right, Steve. For now we'll leave it at that. But if I don't get some answers pretty damn quick I'll want the lady's name. I mean it."

"I appreciate your consideration, Captain. Always a pleasure to deal with the Metropolitan Police."

A slammed receiver was my reply. It made my ear zing as I put down the telephone. So Baldy had been a loogan named Sammy Herod. Interesting information but not sensational. And coming too late to do anyone any good. Zellerhaus's heavy man. I wondered if Larry knew that Sammy was among the departed. And what it would mean to him.

Just then my door bell rang. I wasn't expecting any visitors but it could be a bellhop or the kid from the grocery store with the week's bill. I went over to the door and opened it.

No kid in a butcher's coat and no sharp-eyed bellhop with a telegram on a tip tray. Just a good-looking girl with shoulder-length black hair, long bangs and a chest like Sofia Loren.

Yesterday's heavy turtle-neck sweater had been changed for a low-cut black jersey blouse. The Levis had been left at the pad for a dark skirt. And instead of moccasins, she wore high-heeled black pumps and bare legs. Roxy Bolac.

"Hi, chick," I said. "Where's the rumble?"

She shrugged and sauntered past me. On her face no makeup at all. Only colorless lipstick, Italian style. At her age she could get away with it. Far away. Closing the door, I turned around and watched her.

She was moving toward the sofa in a sinuous flank-rolling walk. Standing, she barely came to my chin, but her legs were tapered and nicely muscled. The Levis had hid all that before. As I stared at her I felt my lips go dry. And something was clotting my throat. She looked older, today, maybe as much as nineteen. But it could have been the grown-up clothes. I didn't really care.

Turning, she sank into the sofa and said, "I'll take scotch."

"Yes, ma'am," I said and went over to the bar. I poured her drink and a duplicate for me. By the time I was handing her the glass she had a cigarette going. From under long lashes her eyes regarded me moodily. She tilted the glass, drank a lot of it and shivered. Then she closed her eyes and shook her head quickly. Opening her eyes again, she blinked, "Man, you build a wicked ball."

"Well," I sighed, "I'm fresh out of tea. Not a stick in the pad. Zilch."

"Leave it," she said throatily. "I dig you're square. You don't have to pretend."

I sipped my drink and sat down on the sofa. "Thoughtful of you to stop by," I observed. "How'd you make me?"

"The license plate," she said boredly. "I got a friend works down at the bureau." She tilted her glass again and finished most of the rest of it. Her cheeks had taken on a little color. I wondered if her hair still smelled of pot. Nuzzling it would be one way to find out. It seemed like an attractive idea. I moved a little closer but she turned and said, "I just came from a funeral. Quinby didn't show. The bastard!"

"Maybe you're expecting too much from him. He could have figured the touch you put on him ended his responsibilities."

Her lips curled slightly. Smoke wisped downward from her nostrils. Her eyes seemed moist. The same angel eyes as her dead sister. In a quiet voice she said, "I though you might have a key to the apartment."

"Why?"

"Peachy and I are—were—the same size. She had some nice threads. I thought I'd take them. Hell, she'd have wanted me to."

I nodded. "Someone went in there last night. Whoever it was tore the place apart. I guess the clothes weren't bothered, though."

Her eyebrows lifted. "The key?"

"Your sister and I weren't on that kind of terms."

Her eyes appraised me. "You would have been," she murmured. "In time."

I took away her glass, made more drinks and carried them back. There was even more color in her face and her tongue dipped into her glass tentatively. I went over to the telephone and asked the switchboard for the janitor's quarters. When Stroud answered I said, "Ray, Miss Bolac's sister is with me. She came by to pick up Miss Bolac's clothing but she doesn't have a key. How about opening the door for her?"

"Yes, suh. Glad to. Right away."

I laid down the phone and went back to Roxy Bolac. She gazed up at me with a gamin expression. "Thanks," she said huskily. "Peachy won't need them any more."

"The rent's paid at least until the end of the month. If you wanted to you could probably move in."

"It might give the Senator ideas."

"Yeah. But you could have the lock changed."

She nodded thoughtfully. "I just might. The pad's getting pretty crowded these nights."

"So I hear."

Her eyebrows drew together. "How?"

"The police," I said. "Fuzz to you."

"It figures." She drank a little more and said, "What do you do for kicks?"

"No bongos. Only a little cool sound from time to time."

Her head turned and she glanced over at the hi-fi cabinet. "Stereo," she murmured. "Like about now, man?"

"Tell you what, before we get any more light-headed, get what you want from Peachy's apartment and come back. I've got to slide out a while but you can make yourself at home. I'll leave the door open."

She stretched, sat forward and finished her drink. Then she got up and wound herself slowly toward the door. One hand grasped the knob and the other reached back and fluffed out her hair. A simple gesture but behind it were a thousand years of artful practice. Turning, she said slowly, "There's something I want to talk about. Like something you should know."

"Like what?" I said. My voice sounded distant, detached. The drinks had socked me hard. My mind was as active as a hibernating snail. The room had taken on an odd angle.

"Like the guy who was always trying to make Peachy and couldn't," she said and went out.

I stared at the partly open door, shook myself and reeled out to the kitchen. I clattered a lot of ice cubes into the sink and covered them with cold water. Dropping a towel in the frigid mixture I let it soak and then I bent over and held it against my face. The cold made lances of pain shoot through my forehead. I gasped, soaked the towel again and applied it once more. This time it felt hotter than a branding iron but it did its work. When I dried my face I was reasonably sober and my brain was functioning again.

I had a purchase to make. It would take half an hour at the most and afterward I would hear what Roxy had to say about Peachy's unsuccessful suitor.

As I entered the living room I pulled up to a sudden stop. I had company. Not Roxy Bolac. Not even a woman.

Company was a tall, lean man with sleek features. He wore a silver-gray summer suit and a matching straw hat, and he looked classier than a tin cornet. I had seen him once before, by night. He was the man who had driven me back from the Zellerhaus country estate. He was Maury Renzo's latest bodyguard.

He stood with his legs spread, balanced and taut. His right hand was out of sight in his coat pocket. I could imagine what it held. I swallowed hard.

"Bentley himself," he purred in an insolent voice. "You get all kinds of special service these days, pal. Even a personal message from Maury."

"Mr. Renzo to you," I said wearily. "And by way of light exercise you might take off the sombrero."

His face tightened and his lips got as thin as sheet steel. I moved forward slowly, stopping about six feet from him. He would want me to stop about there. I didn't want a little thing like distance worrying him. He said, "Hard guy, huh? We might check that out, pal. Some day when I got nothing else to do."

"Look," I said, "I haven't got a world of time. Let's stop the teeth-baring and let it go that you're tougher than me. Anyway, the gun in your pocket says so, and I wouldn't argue for the world. Let's have Maury's message—if you can remember it."

His lips opened and closed. His eyes glinted and he snarled, "Sammy Herod got a carnation pinned on him today. In Quinby's apartment. Maury wants to know how come. He wants to know why and who done it. He wants to know if maybe you did it all by yourself."

"Such a lot of questions," I sighed. "I've got the answers written down somewhere but finding them might take a little time. Some other time, crumb. Dangle."

The hand that had been in his pocket was out now and there was a gun in it. All in a single greased motion. I blinked and licked my lips.

"Talk, pal," he grated. "Talk quick and good."

Behind him the door was opening quietly. I saw a pile of clothes coming into the room, a pair of startled eyes above them. Smiling, I walked toward him and nodded. "I'm ready," I said loudly. "Right now."

Roxy heaved the pile of dresses at the gunman's head. They hit him with a thud and staggered him forward, almost to his knees. He grunted and his hands went down. That neutralized the pistol.

The toe of my left foot connected with his right wrist and he yelped in pain. The gun skidded across the rug. His eyes shot up to my face and as he straightened I slammed my right fist into his jaw. He dropped sideways, hands clawing empty air, but he wasn't out. There was still a bundle of fight left in him. I swerved sideways for the pistol but it wasn't on the rug any longer.

A hand held it, shakily, but pointing at the gunman. While I was entertaining him Roxy had collected it. I stepped over to her, pried it out of her hand and snapped off the safety. It was a Colt .45. Not a parlor pistol. It threw a slug big enough to rip a hole the size of a grapefruit. I told him so.

He stayed on his knees, holding his right wrist and staring at me, a carload of hate in his dark eyes.

I could hear Roxy moving behind me. "Thanks, baby," I husked. "That buys a lot of tea with me."

From the floor the gunman cursed me. I leered at him. "Once more, hard guy," I invited. "I haven't pistol-whipped anyone all day. I'd love to start with you."

CHAPTER FIFTEEN

His left cheek twitched and fear filtered into his eyes. I said, "Where's Maury now?"

"The Marigold," he whinnied.

"Turk Almeida's old place. What's Maury's number?"

He licked his lips and told me. Without taking my eyes from him, I told Roxy to dial it. Then I stepped around the sofa and picked up the receiver with my left hand.

Maury Renzo answered in a terse syllable. I said, "Bentley here. A few minutes ago an uninvited visitor showed up. He went through the tough guy routine with me and mentioned you'd sent him to call. Said you wanted some questions answered."

Renzo said tightly, "I did. What happened to George?"

I moved the phone a couple of inches from my face and said to the gunman, "He's asking for you, George. Mr. Renzo wants to know what happened to you. Now what should I say to that?"

Renzo's voice came as though from a long way off. A brittle, disillusioned voice. "I see. Is George badly damaged?"

"He's in some pain," I said, "but he can walk. He got careless with his iron. I have it in my hand at the moment. I didn't really want it but George sort of forced it on me. Now, what were those questions again?"

Maury Renzo said, "Sammy Herod got plugged today. After what happened the other night it occurred to me you might have had reason to do it."

"I had reason," I grated. "Suppose I drilled Sammy. What would that mean in your busy day?"

"I like things neat, Bentley," he said crisply. "I thought George could handle an inquiry without raising a lot of dust. It seems I was mistaken."

"Badly mistaken," I barked. "George turns out to be another bust. I thought I might break his toys and send him along home. Any objections?"

George's eyes flared hatred.

Maury Renzo spoke again. "Handle it any way you like, Bentley. I take it you didn't get to Sammy."

"I was late," I snapped. "At least an hour late. Any more questions, don't send one of your bolos around to ask them. A phone call costs a dime and it's easier on the hired help."

"So long, Bentley," Maury's voice came. "Don't push your luck."

"I've heard that before," I shot back, but the line had gone dead. I slammed down the phone and rasped, "On your feet, hood. Out. The same way you came."

"The rod," he bleated.

I laughed at him. "The essential item," I jeered. "Like a cobbler's knife."

Pulling out the magazine I snapped the ready cartridge from the chamber. It hit the wall, dropped and spun quietly on the strip of bare flooring. To George I said, "You could have gunned Sammy yourself. Nothing says you didn't."

He swallowed hard and his eyes ate the empty Colt in my hand. Suddenly I threw it at him. It hit his chest and he scrabbled for it with his good hand. The Colt disappeared into his left pocket. Then he spun around, grabbed up his hat and loped toward the doorway.

"Guns," I muttered after him. "Some guys think a gun in the hand gives them diplomatic immunity."

George whirled around and whinnied, "Without the dame you couldn'ta taken me."

"Without the gun you wouldn't have braced me, hood. They don't call them equalizers for nothing."

He disappeared into the hallway, a lean, wolfish tocker with maybe a chipped wristbone as a souvenir.

Roxy was gathering the dresses together. I stuck the Colt magazine in a drawer, and began helping her. When we had them all piled on the sofa I said, "That was cool, baby. I kind of liked the way you sized things up."

Her eyes petted me. Her lips wore the trace of a smile. "For a square you looked pretty good yourself."

"For a square," I said, and reached out and got hold of her.

She came into the clinch as easily as a key in the right tumbler. If she was young in years she was ancient in intuition.

Her eyelids fluttered and closed. Her mouth opened against mine and her breath was a hot searching wind. I felt her tongue uncoil until it was probing the sensitive part behind my upper lip. Our hands were like hungry animals exploring for food. One of mine nosed along her spine and I felt a shudder start at her toes and work all the way up to the top of her scalp. She didn't push her breasts against me or grind her loins like a harlot. She didn't need to. It was all there, along with an unspoken understanding of what life's big chase was all about. Unfortunately it would have to wait. I nibbled her tongue lightly and murmured, "You said you came from where?"

She drew back and studied me with smoldering eyes. "Easton, Pa. Only I didn't say."

"It must be quite a town," I mused. "Easton, Pa. I never would have thought it. Well, we'll talk it over later. Right now I gotta slide."

"Don't make it too much later," she said huskily. "I wouldn't want to drift too far out."

"Hold down the fort, dreamboat. I've got to parley with the natives."

"You'll bring back some loot?"

"Anything your little heart desires."

"Don't linger, lover." She nibbled the point of my chin.

"Keep the home fires burning," I croaked in a voice like burlap and tottered toward the door. Opening it, I managed to make my way down the corridor without stumbling even once.

Examining myself in the elevator mirror, I murmured the praises of colorless lipstick and wondered why something so obviously practical hadn't been invented generations before. And it had taken a beatnik sex-pot to put me hip.

Down in the basement garage I saw old Barney puttering around his office. There was a big bandage on the back of his head, a souvenir of Sammy Herod's work. Possibly the last known sample. Barney saw me and waved a hand weakly. Normally he would have helped unravel my Olds from the tight slot where it was parked, but he was making a good thing out of the bandage. I doubted that Sammy had busted him any harder than he had me but I was managing to stagger through my appointed rounds without asking for special consideration.

It took me about five minutes to work the Olds up the ramp and point north toward Chevy Chase. Rush-hour traffic was over and I had most of three lanes to myself. It was lucky because I had to keep the needle right on the maximum to reach the store before it closed.

It was set between a liquor shop and a Chinese restaurant with green and red dragons painted on the windows and oriental-style gold lettering. A dusty window card advertised family-style Chinese dinners and invited wedding and banquet business. Maybe they even got some.

The shop had only one sidewalk window and that jammed with hi-fi amplifiers and speaker cabinets plus an assortment of beach radios and TV sets.

The guy behind the counter wore overalls and a blue work shirt. His hands were stained with soldering flux. A small business where you had to double in electronic service to keep going. He seemed pleased to see me when I came in, but he must have figured me for a TV sale because when I told him what I wanted he began to frown. I reminded him that he was listed as a distributor.

"Yeah," he said. "I got a franchise but hell, I only unload about one set a year. A spare tape spool you wanted? Not sure I even got one." He went into the back of his shop and I could hear boxes being pushed and dragged around. After a while he came out with a little plastic spool in his hand. "This isn't a spare, mister. I took it from a set. By the time I sell the set I'll be able to order another from New York." He began writing up the sale. "Five-eighty," he said. "Plus tax."

I paid him, waved off the receipt and pocketed the little spool. The tape on it was dark green. The trip out had been worthwhile. Anyone who had seen the original spool—the missing one—wouldn't have been fooled by a spare wound with American brown tape. And the whole idea was to fool someone.

Turning the Olds around, I headed across Western Avenue to Wisconsin and down toward Georgetown. Neon bar signs were flickering on and grocers were sweeping shopping litter from their sidewalks in the last fading light. The pulse of traffic had died away and honest folk were taking up the threads of family living. Togetherness. Ma, Pa and the kids clustered around the giant tube, squabbling over the channel while the TV dinners thawed in the oven.

I crossed Macomb Street and Woodley Road. Then down past the big Gothic cathedral, Mount Alto hospital, Holy Rood cemetery and on into Georgetown. Turning west on Volta Place, I cruised past the white Seventh Precinct station and parked a block from Alma's salt-box.

The carriage lamps glowed as I walked up to the door and rang the bell. A properly outfitted maid answered the door and asked me what I wanted in an accent I had come to recognize. I told her my name and asked for Miss Ward. She said she would see if Miss Ward was home, and closed the door. I shook out a cigarette, stuck it in my jaw and chewed it.

After a while the maid came back and invited me inside. She closed the door behind me and I followed her out to the terrace. The only illumination came from candles in two hurricane lamps on the wrought-iron table. I could see their reflection in the archway mirrors at the far end of the garden. Birds were fluttering invisibly in the locust trees overhead and the light scent of jasmine had started to infiltrate the terrace. I sat down, lighted my cigarette and waited. The maid brought out a silver tray with the right bottles on it and offered me a drink. I settled for a glass of iced soda. It seemed out of character, but I had belted down my share of sauce earlier in the day and recent events indicated that I might need my wits about me after nightfall. The knuckles of my right hand throbbed. A little souvenir of George. By now he had gone scuttling back to Maury Renzo. If all he got was a tongue-lashing he would be a very lucky hoodlum.

The screen door opened and Alma Ward stepped out onto the terrace. She was wearing a dark dress, dark shoes and no visible jewelry. She said, "Steve, I thought we'd settled this. Why do you persist in trying to upset things?"

"Calm down, angel," I said and gestured at a chair. "I guess you know a dead man named Sammy Herod was found in the Senator's apartment this afternoon."

She sat down and adjusted her skirt. A trifle irritably, I thought. "I read something of the sort on the office teletype. Except the Senator's apartment wasn't identified."

"That was thoughtful," I muttered. "The immunity of those in high places."

"Not for long," she said scornfully, got up and began making herself a drink. "I suppose you know you've arrived at an inconvenient time. Or possibly that's why you chose this moment to arrive." She sampled her drink, made a face and went back to her chair. Crossing her legs carefully, she gazed at me.

I said, "A while back we were speculating that you might not get further instructions tonight. In that case we would know that

Sammy Herod had been Peachy's killer and the man who offered you the recording."

She nodded. "I'm hoping otherwise."

"I know that. You want the tape. That's where your interest begins and ends. What happens to the killer doesn't matter to you."

She spread her hands. "We've gone through this before. I want to see justice done, of course. But in this case, getting the tape takes priority over anything else."

"Money ready?" I sipped cold soda and stared at her.

"Of course," she said petulantly. "I've had it ready since yesterday."

"Always the practical girl," I observed. "You don't care from whom you buy the recording, do you?"

"Of course not," she snapped. "Steve, you're getting awfully tedious."

"Swell," I said. "You'd buy it from anyone. Supposing I had it, Alma. You'd buy it from me?"

"I suppose so. But that's ridiculous. That would make you the murderer."

"Not necessarily. First off you don't know that the man who's been calling you actually has—or has ever had—possession of the recording. For all you know he may have thought he could get it when he needed it—perhaps by exhuming the recorder from wherever Peachy had hidden it. Her apartment was ransacked last night, by the way. Probably by Sammy Herod. We found the recorder with him today remember, but that's circumstantial evidence." I sipped from my glass again. "The spool was missing from the recorder but again that's no proof that the man who offered to sell it ever had it or has it now. Let's suppose he had the reel once, but it got out of his possession between yesterday and today. The fact that he no longer has anything to sell you wouldn't prevent him from trying to get your eight grand. A defenseless woman on a lonely road is fairly easy prey for a man who's killed once and maybe twice."

Something crossed her face. For the first time, doubt seemed to be troubling her. Then her chin lifted and she said breathily, "I don't believe it."

"You don't believe it because you don't want to believe it. You've banked on it happening the way you planned and you don't even want to consider the possibility that there's room for an error in judgment. Your judgment."

Lifting her wrist, she moved it toward the candlelight and read the dial of her watch. "It's almost time for the call," she said carefully. "When it comes one of your questions will be answered."

I got up, splashed more soda into my glass, added an ice cube and sat down again. The candlelight made Alma's face look paler than usual. She had penciled her eyebrows carefully and her lips were twin bows of red. All for a killer's delectation.

I said, "Seen Jay lately?"

Her lips drew together, then parted. "Not since yesterday. Why?"

"I wonder where he is right now," I said idly. "I suppose you've considered the possibility that the man who called you is your husband."

Flesh shrank against the bones of her face. Her eyes opened and closed. Her tongue flicked out and moistened her lips. "It couldn't be Jay," she whispered.

"Why not? Jay had access to Peachy's apartment. If he didn't kill her he could always have gone there and taken the tape recorder. In his position money means quite a lot. Turning the recording over to his Committee would get him nothing more than a moist handshake from the Chairman. Whereas, by selling it to you he'd collect eight grand and still see Quinby laid by the heels. Not by the Committee but by public opinion. From his point of view it might just add up to the same thing." I sat forward and put down my glass. "The point is you haven't a clue to the identity of the man you've been dealing with. Now that you've thought about it you realize it could be Jay himself. And in addition to the cash return the additional satisfaction of flummoxing a supercilious wife might be irresistible."

Her hands framed her face. "I ... I don't know what to think. It was all very clear until you came here. All you've done is confuse me."

"Never an easy task," I said and looked down at the dial of my wristwatch. "Time for the phone to ring."

We both sat there straining to listen. The terrace was so quiet I could hear soft wax dripping on the base of the mantel.

Then like a dam ripping asunder the telephone sounded. Before the first ring had died away Alma was on her feet. She darted into the house and I could hear her running feet. Alma reached the phone before the maid, and I could hear her say excitedly, "Yes ... yes, this is Miss Ward. Of course. I remember your voice. Yes, I'm prepared to follow instructions. I have the money ready." Then her voice dropped away as though she was listening.

I pushed out of my chair and walked down the stone steps into the garden. Turning, I looked back at the terrace, the candlelight reflecting dimly in the windows. A peaceful scene. I dug one toe into the earth to give myself a sense of reality. Then I dug my hand into the pocket and gripped the little reel of tape I had bought earlier.

Alma came out sooner than I expected, handbag over one arm, and pulling on her gloves nervously. "I'm leaving, Steve," she said unsteadily. "Wish me luck."

I walked toward her and mounted the steps. Her lips were trembling but her face was set and her eyes glinted like black glass. Full of determination and ready for adventure.

"You said you'd buy the reel from anyone, Alma. Even from me."

"Steve—that's quite enough. Can't you see I'm in a hurry?"

"Even from me," I repeated and lifted the little reel from my pocket. Walking closer, I laid it in her hand. "Save yourself a trip, beautiful. Pay me the eight thousand instead."

CHAPTER SIXTEEN

er eyes widened and her mouth opened. I thought she was going to scream. Instead her right hand lifted and pressed hard against her mouth. She took a step backward, her eyes fixed on mine, and then she began to shake. I grabbed her shoulders and shook her hard. The hand fell away from her mouth. *"You,"* she hissed. *"Where did you get it?"*

"A new moon but an old refrain. Eight thousand, please. That was the price mentioned."

Her face was a study in horror and bafflement. "Where ... where did you get it?" Her eyes flickered down to the reel, then back to my face. "Today—in the apartment. You got it then. It was in the recorder all the time. And you let me think—"

"—What you wanted to." I added some gravel to my voice. "What's the matter, Alma? The article's for sale. Don't you want it?"

Her mouth opened and closed. Then she seemed to pull herself together. Abruptly her free hand opened her purse, plunged in and handed me a thick paper envelope. Then she dropped the little reel into her purse and snapped it shut. Her head lifted and her nostrils dilated. "You've got your money. That's what you wanted, wasn't it?"

"And you've got the reel. That's what you wanted. But I still need one thing more."

"Yes?"

"The contact instructions," I said, fitting the envelope into my inside pocket. "Where, when and how."

One hand lifted distractedly and fingered a strand of hair. "The Jefferson Memorial," she breathed. "In half an hour. I was to park on the Tidal Basin curve with both windows open. Another car would pull alongside and toss a package through my window. Then I was to hand over the envelope."

"Nothing more. No signals?"

She nodded slowly. "My brake lights were to be on."

"I'll need your car."

She seemed to draw together. "Steve, please...let it go the way it is."

"You know I can't. Give me the keys."

Slowly, mechanically, she opened her purse and took out a key ring. In a leaden voice she said, "It's parked on 34th Street halfway down the block." Her hand slid into her purse again and she drew out the little reel. "I wonder," she mused. "You know I need another recorder to listen to this, but there's no place open to buy one until tomorrow. You knew that. Why couldn't you have given it to me earlier?"

"Maybe I wanted to see if you'd really go through with it."

"I told you I would."

"You had guts enough, I'll give you that." My hand closed over hers and took away the key ring. "Thanks for everything, beautiful. As someone was saying earlier: wish me luck."

She nodded slightly. I moved past her, opened the screen door and crossed through the house. Opening the front door, I let it swing shut behind me. It closed with a clatter like a coffin lid dropping into place.

The cobbled street was dark. The old-fashioned street lights glowed like miner's lamps. I found the Olds, opened it and groped inside the glove compartment. The Walther was there, still wrapped in its protective flannel. I peeled it away, jacked a shell into the chamber and shoved the pistol into its holster. Then I locked the Olds and walked the rest of the way back to 34th Street and down the block to where Alma's Riley was parked.

I was standing on the curb, stooping over and fitting the key into the door lock, when I heard motion behind me. Whirling, I saw a man step out of the hedge shadow and come toward me. What light there was showed me his face, a short-sleeved shirt and a cap. There was a wide black belt around his hips with a black leather holster and a cartridge clip. The silver-colored badge on his cap glinted dully.

"This your car, mister?"

"No, officer."

"What you plan to do with it?"

"Drive it around the block to the Texaco station. Like the lady asked."

He pondered it a while and then he said, "I guess that'll be okay. My orders only concerned Mrs. Redpath."

"What sort of orders?"

"Not for me to say. She in her house?"

"Five minutes ago she was."

He nodded as though that pleased him.

I said, "In case she took a drive tonight she'd have company. A black Ford with special plates and a whip aerial long enough for a tuna boat."

"Something like that," he admitted. "Guess I'll drop by and see if the lady has any complaints to make. Plenty of prowlers on the loose. Lady living alone needs protection."

Turning back, I opened the Riley door and slid inside. "There's also a German maid with flaxen hair and a turned-up nose," I told him. "I'll bet she's got a spare chunk of strudel just waiting for you."

"Thanks for the tip." He spun his nightstick and sauntered off.

Kellaway's work, I thought. Stopping up the mouse-holes.

The Riley was an export model with left-hand steering and fluid drive. The motor purred like a basket of happy kittens and I swung away from the curb. I drove down to Q Street, crossed

Wisconsin and turned up 31st. Parking in front of a huge Victorian house I got out and walked up to the porch.

When the Negro maid came to the door I asked her if I might see Mrs. Jeanette Ward.

"Mrs. Ward is giving a dinner party. Is it important?"

"To me it is. Let's let her decide."

The door closed and I thought about lighting a cigarette to amuse myself during what might be a considerable wait. But my mouth was too dry and my tongue tasted like the floor of a bus station. I patted the Walther underneath my thin coat, leaned against the doorway and waited. After a while the door opened and the maid asked me to step inside. She showed me to a reception room on the right and went away. There were chairs enough if anyone wanted to sit down and an oval table topped with black marble big enough for ice hockey. Then the doors opened and Mrs. Ward came in, silver-knobbed stick in her right hand. Peering at me through a lorgnette, she snapped, "The maid said this was important, young man. I hope it is. I'm entertaining a very distinguished group this evening and I abhor a hostess absenting herself."

I said, "What I wanted to see you about is important to me. It also has to do with Alma."

"Speak up. Don't take all evening to tell me."

I pulled the money envelope from my pocket and laid it on the black table top. "A little while ago Alma gave me some money, Mrs. Ward. I didn't really want it, but I took it to prevent her getting into a position of danger. My taking it was the convincer that changed her mind. In the morning I'd like you to return it to her."

"Yes. I will. What else?" Her lips bit off the words as sharply and accurately as a coin-stamping machine.

"I'd like another envelope, please—an unused one—a few sheets of newspaper and a pair of scissors. The maid can bring me that while you go back to your guests."

She shuffled forward, her left hand picked up the envelope and she said in a softer voice, "I haven't the faintest idea what this is about or what you may be up to. But I have the feeling I should be thanking you for something. I'll have the maid bring you what you want."

"Thank you, Mrs. Ward."

She lifted her cane, inscribed a circle with her fist and barked, "Oh, bosh! I have made inquiries about you, young man, and I found that General Ballou knows you and thinks highly of you. He mentioned that you once had been involved in a delicate matter in his behalf."

"It was kind of the General to remember me."

"There was something about his daughter, Frances. You were in love with her?"

"Miss Ballou lives in the south of France," I said. "Her daughter is with her and they seem happy there. I haven't seen her in nearly two years."

"I see," she said quietly. "Good night, Steven."

"Good night, ma'am."

She extended one bony hand and I took it. It felt as frail as a newly hatched chicken and the veins looked like strands of purple wool. Turning briskly she shuffled through the doorway. I could hear her talking to the maid and then the far doors opened and for a moment I could hear voices in conversation, the sound of silver on good china and the delicate chime of crystal. The doors closed and silence took over.

When the maid came back she brought what I had asked for and left me alone. I cut strips of newspaper the size of currency and trimmed them into a stack. Then I fitted them into the envelope and sealed it. The envelope I put inside my coat pocket. Everything else I left on the black marble table and walked out into the dim hallway.

The maid opened the door for me, said good night and I stepped out onto the porch.

Tall elms hid the moon as I got back into the Riley. I started the engine, turned around and headed south toward Rock Creek Parkway.

The dash held a small, efficient-looking British radio but I didn't turn it on. It might have provided comfort but at the same time it could have distracted me from things I had to concentrate on.

I was to park the Riley on the water side of Jefferson Memorial and put on the brake lights. Then with the windows rolled down I was to wait for a car to come alongside, stop and toss a package through my window. A package presumably containing the missing reel. In exchange I was to hand over an envelope presumably containing eight thousand dollars. I wondered if either of us would get what he was expecting.

The identity of the driver of the other car was the key to the whole thing. Unless the killer was cautious enough to send around a delivery boy on a bike. What I didn't like was the sequence of events. In most blackmail or payoff transactions the side with the goods wants to see the color of your money before delivery is made. The way this exchange had been set up, Alma was to get possession of the reel before handing over the cash. That could be either sloppy figuring on the killer's part, inexperience, or a touching faith in human honesty. At the least it made him seem unprofessional. Sammy Herod wouldn't have done it that way, nor George the handsome hoodlum. But neither of them was likely to show up. Sammy was dead and George was probably out of commission for the next week. That limited the possibilities, but not enough. There were still interested parties to spare, plus potential intermediaries, but I was hoping it wouldn't all collapse into something as useless as a kid on a bike, running an errand for someone he didn't know and couldn't contact directly.

Less than ten minutes to go. The Riley was humming along the wide blacktop highway, curving smoothly past the *Titanic* Memorial where one night a million years ago I had nuzzled the kid sister of a Spanish Baroness, now dead. Past the Bryan Monument, William Jennings, not Joe, and along above the Watergate amphitheater where they used to hold concerts on summer nights. Now killed by popularity—like burlesque.

Seconds more and I could see the calm glitter of the Tidal Basin, and beyond, on its south rim, the high pillared cupola of Thomas Jefferson's memorial. Clouds gave the moon a tattered look as though the rats of heaven had been gnawing their silver cheese. Not far from Mexico City there was a giant Pyramid of the Moon that I had climbed once. I remembered the steep lava block sides, the broiling sun on my back.... I shook myself, my mind was drifting away to inconsequentials. Sitting forward, I hunched over the wheel and saw the big moon-white memorial glide past on my left.

Slowing I saw that there was only a sparse concentration of parked cars. It was early enough that the Park Police were willing to presume nothing illicit was going on behind their darkened windows. The heavy work came later, after cabarets and saloons closed down. Whoever he was, the killer had picked a good hour and a good rendezvous to conclude his business.

Off to my right lay Washington Chanel with my ketch bobbing at its buoy, anonymous among dozens of other white-painted summer craft. The hoot of a steamboat whistle announced the departure of the night boat for Old Point Comfort. A couple of nights from now Mrs. Bross would be on it with high hopes and a new permanent. Whether she would have a job to return to depended on the next quarter of an hour.

Slowing the Riley, I pulled the Walther from its holster. Laying it on the seat beside me, I snapped off the safety and got out the sealed envelope of newspapers. Then I put the envelope beside the pistol and loosened my tie. My pulse had begun to pound and sweat was trickling down the side of my nose. I wiped it away, blinked and peered at my watch. Only five minutes to go.

I didn't want to arrive at the rendezvous so far ahead of time that the killer could cruise past me and learn that someone other than Alma Ward was behind the wheel.

I thought of Quinby and Zellerhaus and Jay Redpath and Nagle and dead Sammy Herod. I thought of George and Maury Renzo and the Marigold Club over the District line where I had put the snub on Turk Almeida. I thought of dead men and flower-banked coffins, of a girl strangled by a silk stocking in a bedroom next to mine. Of the final velvet curtain that drops for all men born of women. Death was a marble slab in the morgue and the reek of preservative. Honor was an old soldier on a park bench staring at nothing. Compromise was somewhere in between.

The bridge was below me. I crossed it slowly, came to a turn-around and started back. The Riley responded like a slave girl to the Sultan's touch. A sleek car, as machined and capable as its mistress. I thought about Alma and wondered if she had stayed home as I planned she should. Or if she had decided to do something quixotic and futile. Like calling the police.

The stand of Yoshino cherry trees was beginning on my right, the Memorial turnoff just ahead. Beyond a grove of trees a white marking line and a metal arrow showed the way.

I slowed the Riley to a crawl, like any rubberneck tourist or a wolf with a hot little bunny beside him. Between the parked cars there was plenty of distance. Finding space for the Riley would be no problem.

My right hand touched the Walther and hefted it. It was as cold and heavy as a winter tombstone. I licked dry lips and sat back against the seat to keep my profile small and indeterminate. Clouds covered the shopworn moon. The Tidal Basin was as black and smooth as onyx. Stiff hands turned the Riley along the circular drive, eased it into an open area on the water side.

Pulling out the hand brake lighted the tail lamps but I kept the motor running. The other car would make its approach on the left side. I crawled over next to the right-hand door, gathered the pistol in my hand and picked up the envelope with my left hand. From where I sat I would be hard to see unless the other driver lighted my face.

About a minute to go, my watch said. If the other man was punctual. He didn't have to come alongside by car, of course. Already he could have parked farther away and hidden himself in the shrubbery, ready to approach from the curb side. In any case, the stage was set.

A car was coming from behind me. I felt myself stiffen and my trigger finger twitched against the trigger guard. My left fingers rasped the envelope. The contents seemed as heavy as sheet bronze.

As the car neared I shrank farther into the shadowed corner, but it cruised on by and I saw that it held two couples. No killer there. Air whistled through my teeth as I blew out my lungs. Then I sucked in a deep breath and felt myself shiver.

My gun hand seemed coated with fish slime but it was only nervous sweat. I saw headlights in the rearview mirror. Dim lights that showed nothing of the car's make or model. It came on, hesitantly, I thought, as though the driver were weaving curiously back and forth from the curbing. Slower it came, still slower, and veering almost at the rear of the Riley. Then at the last moment it swerved out and idled to a stop.

My left arm was taut, ready to loft the envelope into the other car. My straining eyes saw a hand appear on the door sill of the other car. The wrist made a flicking motion and something sailed through my window. Something dark and the size of a giant lemon. It hit the dash with a heavy metallic sound and glanced onto the floor. Too heavy for a spool of tape. The heel of my gun hand hit the door release and I spilled out frantically onto soft grass. I heard a jeering call behind me and as I lunged for the shelter of a tree the earth blew apart.

CHAPTER SEVENTEEN

Yellow-orange flame spat through the sky and metal slammed into the tree trunk. A tornado rushed past me and I heard the Riley lift and settle heavily on its axles. The other car was only twenty yards ahead, outlined by the burning Riley, when I sprinted after it, knelt on the curb and shot.

The Walther seemed to leap toward the rear of the other car. It was gathering speed now. I shot again and then a third time. The last shot found the gas tank and flame spurted into the night. The other car hit the curb awkwardly and began rolling down the embankment. A door opened and a figure leaped free.

I didn't need moonlight to see him now. The light around him was brilliant. I knelt and aimed. The Walther jumped in my hand but the shot led him too much. I fired again and saw him spin wildly and lurch forward. Just then the other car went over the bank into the Tidal Basin, its flames snuffed out by the water that surged over it.

Shakily I got to my feet and began walking over to to him. My legs were stiffer than cement poles. From ten yards away I could hear him moaning but the light from the Riley's flames was too far away to show his face. His hands were clawing at his hip, tearing at his clothing, his groans were hoarse with agony.

There were headlights along the circle now, the ruckus of car engines frantically starting, the scream of tire rubber against pavement. I walked leadenly onward, the barrel of my pistol pointing at the fallen man's heart.

Then from behind me I heard the rising wail of a siren. Two cars flashed past me, then a third, engines straining to make distance. A lance of pain shot through my right knee and I almost stumbled. Gritting my teeth, I kept on.

The siren was getting closer, a spotlight hit my back, lighted the tortured face of the man on the ground. I was close enough. Stopping, I felt myself begin to totter. The dizziness must have come from holding my breath because when I filled my lungs I steadied. The siren behind me was only a drifting growl now, and I could hear the thud of feet running toward me. An arm grabbed me roughly and a voice roared, "Who is he?"

"Nagle," I husked and turned around. "Lester Nagle. Someone Captain Kellaway's been looking for."

"Yeah?" the voice jeered. "You'll get your chance to talk to Kellaway."

I shook off the policeman's hand. It grabbed for my Walther and snatched it away. Other hands and arms hustled me around and shoved me toward the open door of a prowl car. As I sank onto the seat I could see the Riley burning in the rear-view mirror.

The clock high on the office wall was the electric government-issue model that never shows the right time. It was nearly fifteen minutes slow. The watch on my wrist showed ten-thirty even. The Venetian blinds were closed, showing grimy, paint-peeled metal. On a radiator box, half-hidden by shadows, stood a low oval dish, banked with green moss and holding a Japanese dwarf tree. Ginger or persimmon. I could never remember which. Possibly a mental block.

The man who owned it sat behind his desk. The pencil in his hand made scratching sounds on a pad of yellow ruled paper. Also government issue. The top of his desk held a litter of soggy coffee containers. The two ash trays had overflowed onto the desk and the circulating fan in the corner scattered ashes over the yellow pad.

Until a few minutes ago the room had been noisily crowded. Police stenographers, laboratory men and junior cops taking in a wrap-up. I had gotten hoarse from talking and now my throat ached. Black coffee well laced with alcohol was something I could have used a quart of. But policemen don't give that stuff away. The room held the rancid stench of sweaty shirts and stale tobacco, the echo of tough cynical voices. It would always hold the stench and the echo; it was a policeman's office.

My knee had gone stiff and my right cheekbone ached. I told Kellaway so.

He glanced up and said, "Count your blessings, Kiddo. The grenade Nagle tossed could have blasted you into ten pounds of bloody hamburger. Your lady's car's a total loss, of course. Not to mention Nagle's heap."

I mumbled something about the Riley.

Kellaway chewed the end of his pencil. "One thing we'll both remember—a Riley's a fast car to get out of. That grenade only had a four-second fuse. With your winged feet you oughta try for the Olympics."

"I like Washington," I said. "A nice quiet town to grow old in."

His eyebrows lifted. "You? Hell, you'll never hit forty. Not standing up."

I closed my eyes and tried to find a soft spot on the wooden seat. The hope was as false as a lover's promise.

The scratching noise stopped. Kellaway cleared his throat, hawked into the spittoon and chimed a ringer. He said, "I haven't liked this from the start. Not any of it. I haven't liked the way you played fast and loose with me, not to mention the truth, the lengths you went to and the chances you took." He lifted my pistol from his blotter, sighted along the barrel, said, "Blam, blam," and laid it down again.

"It's eating me to a husk," I said. "The guy tried to kill me. What was I supposed to do? Saunter down here and write out a complaint while he piled up the miles between us?"

Kellaway shrugged. "You weren't supposed to do anything at all. You weren't supposed to have been there tonight baiting the trap. All that was police business." He hefted the Walther again. "Not bad shooting, if I say so myself. A gas tank and a killer in five shots."

"There was more light than a TV studio," I said in a raw voice. "A kid couldn't have missed."

"Plenty of troopers might have missed."

"Nagle's car was an old job—the tank stood out like a palm tree in the desert."

He eyed me curiously. "What the hell, you getting genteel in your old age, Stevie? We sound like a couple college classmates beering it up on their fortieth reunion."

"Hardly that," I said. "Just my way of letting you know I realize I didn't handle things entirely by the rule book."

"You want a big spitty kiss?"

I started to shake my head but it hurt too much. "Just my gun," I told him. "I'll settle for that. You don't even have to return the slug in Nagle's hip."

He lifted the gun, leaned across the desk and handed it to me. I opened my coat and slid the pistol into its holster.

He stared at the bulge by my shoulder and shook his head. "You're one guy who works a permit overtime. For you they oughta double the annual fee."

I was working on something to say but the phone rang then and while Kellaway talked I squirmed my haunches around and tried to get comfortable. Finally he clanged down the phone and said, "From Nagle's apartment. They found the tape reel there, where he said it was. In a hollowed-out book of French poems." He shook his head. "That ain't all they found. Lester had a pornographic library it'll take us a week to burn."

"After you've all leered through it," I wheezed.

He looked at me and frowned. "One of the silent types, Nagle. Timid. Maybe even a mother complex. Then all of a sudden it flared up and he hadda have a woman. That was Loris Bolac's bad luck."

"Probably she didn't take him seriously," I said. "Everyone figured him for a panz."

"Yeah. Well, they say there's some of it in all of us. Effeminate and a rape-murderer. Jesus Christ!"

"That's how I wrote him off," I said. "On the other hand, plenty of signs pointed to Nagle. The killer had to be someone who knew about Angel Eyes and someone who had reason to protect Quinby. On one plane Nagle disapproved of Quinby's love nest and feared the sort of publicity that might come from it. On the other level he lusted after Quinby's woman. So he raped her and on the way out collected the tape reel and Quinby's photograph. Satisfying pent-up drives and protecting his boss—also a distant relative."

Kellaway opened his desk drawer, pulled out a ten-cent cigar and bit off the end. He didn't light it. He stuck it in his mouth and stared at me over the tip. He said, "The way Nagle tells it Sammy Herod tried to see the Senator and show him the recorder Sammy found in Peachy's apartment. Sammy probably thought it was what everyone was looking for. But the Senator had ducked town and Nagle arranged to meet him in the Senator's apartment. Nagle says he panicked when he saw the recorder again and figured Sammy was wise. So he shot him and left him there, intending to take the body out after dark and dump it some place over the line. You figure it that way?"

"No. I figured Sammy thought he had something salable and tried to put the bite on Quinby—or someone else."

"They've test-fired Nagle's thirty-two and the slug matches the one we pulled out of Sammy's skull. So either way it adds up to the same thing. At this point, who the hell cares? Nagle can only step off once."

I stood up as creakily as an antique rocker and steadied myself on the desk. "One final item."

He looked up suspiciously. "Yeah? Like what?"

"You've got your killer. You can close your books on two cases. You're Homicide. The things Senators and lobbyists sometimes do isn't your department. It isn't necessarily police business at all."

His teeth clamped into the cigar and it crackled like dry straw. His lips drew back and closed around the cigar end. There was a sour look on his face. "So what?" he said finally.

"So this: you've got a reel of tape and so have I. Let's trade."

His eyes flickered and his right hand balled into a fist. "You got the reel here?"

"I can get it tonight."

He said nothing. The cigar moved from one side of his mouth to the other. Finally he leaned forward heavily, pressed the intercom lever and barked an order. I tried to flex my right knee. It moved a little. After a hot shower and a night's sleep it might do even better.

A uniformed policeman came in with a small cardboard exhibit box. He handed it to Kellaway and went out. When the door had snicked shut Kellaway lifted the top off the box, removed a white tag from the reel and handed it to me. "I'll need the other one in the morning," he said quietly. "If this'll hang Quinby by the thumbs it's yours with love."

"It will," I said and dropped it into my coat pocket.

The clock on the wall said ten-thirty now. I mentioned it to Kellaway. "Hell," he rasped. "I'm used to it by now. Sort of like my old man. He had a gold railroad watch he always kept one hour and twelve minutes fast. The only reason he ever gave me was protection against pickpockets." He fumbled at his trouser pocket and drew out a worn gold watch. "See? Set just the way he left it."

"Good night, Captain," I said. "Sweet dreams."

He scowled at me as I limped around the end of the desk. "You figure we work an eight-hour day in Homicide? The reports I got to write, I'll be lucky if I hit bed by dawn."

"It was only a figure of speech," I croaked over my shoulder, opened the door and went out.

I made it down the long corridor slower than usual but I wasn't in any particular hurry. People were either home or they weren't. What I could do about it from here was zero.

The outside air was stuffy but it was cleaner and less smoke-laden than what I had been breathing in Kellaway's office. I filled my lungs with it, hobbled down the steps and leaned against a parking meter until a cruising cab spotted me and stopped.

I got in and sank back against the cushions. The cab pulled away, idling until I had given an address. As we bumped over Volta Place's cobblestones I saw my Olds parked where I had left it. On the corner a patrolman stood under a street light and rapped his stick against the base. Sounding for treasure, maybe, or just giving himself enough self-confidence to finish out his beat down Georgetown's dark alleys.

I paid the cabbie and pried myself out of the door. The cab rolled away and I walked up the sidewalk to an entrance framed by glowing bull's-eye carriage lanterns. I pushed the button and stifled a yawn. The way I felt an ounce of alcohol would rocket me out beyond Mars.

I pressed the button again and after a while someone tugged the door inward. Not the Bremerhaven lass but a lady in a long silk gown, hair falling low around her shoulders. I heard a quick intake of breath and then the door opened wider. I went in.

Propping myself against the end of the sofa, I said, "Sorry about the hour and all that, but the hunt's over. I thought you'd want to know."

Her head moved wonderingly. "After all you've been through that's all you have to say? I heard it on TV an hour ago. You were nearly killed." She moved forward and her hand touched the bruise on my cheek. "Don't you want a drink?"

"Maybe a cup of sack posset," I mumbled. "Nothing stronger."

"I'm sorry," she said worriedly, "I'm afraid I—"

"Still got the reel I gave you?"

"Of course."

"It was blank," I said. "I bought it myself." My hand came out of my pocket and showed her the other one. "This is what you bought, sweetheart. The one Nagle found and kept."

Her eyes stared at it like the eyes of a fascinated bird. Her voice grew taut. "You got it from Nagle?" she whispered.

"Who cares where it came from? Give me the other one and we'll call it quits. Your money, by the way, is at your mother's house."

"I know," she said quietly. "Mother called me not long after you left. I went there and got it." Her lips brushed my cheek. "I know why you did that, darling. It was in case you didn't get back."

"Buttercups," I said as lightly as I could, and then her arms went around me and her lips covered mine. When we finally broke apart she said, "Nagle would have killed me tonight."

"No," I said. "He called here from a filling station on Wisconsin. Two minutes later he was parked where he could see who got into the Riley. He saw me, not you. So I wasn't as clever as I thought."

She turned then, crossed to an antique desk and opened a locked drawer. When she came back she handed me the little reel I had bought out in Chevy Chase. Tomorrow it would be in Kellaway's office. "Thanks," I said. "Quinby's all yours now. Go get him."

"I will," she said, and her eyes flashed. "And Zellerhaus, too."

"Sorry about the Riley, but I guess it's insured. There'll be a bill or two you can pay. Small stuff, though. My time goes for free."

She nodded, then moved close to me again. "The maid's sleeping in tonight, Steve, but you can stay if you want to. It's just that in the morning—"

I put one finger over her lips. "Why complicate life? Besides, I've got a little missionary work left to do tonight."

Her eyebrows arched. "Over a fallen young woman?"

"Possibly. Call me in a couple of weeks—when the TV show's behind you and we can have a quiet drink in the garden."

"Sooner than that, darling. You know all this has cut me pretty deeply."

"Like a scratch on a steel door."

She gave me a brave little smile. I turned and walked away.

I made it slowly to the Olds, over the ancient polished cobble-stones, unlocked the door and slid inside. Down the street a pair of gaslights flickered in front of someone's steps. The light was white and thin, like spirit lamps from another age. I turned the ignition key and the engine roared into life. In the quiet street it sounded like the grenade exploding in Alma's Riley. I shuddered and gripped the wheel hard. Then I pulled away from the curb and turned north on 35th.

Along Wisconsin the late movies were letting out and the saloons were doing overflow business. Massachusetts was slumbering and there was none of the commercial gaudiness I had just passed. Down in the basement garage the night car washer was soaping down a car and whistling above the rush of water. When I eased out of the Olds he touched his cap visor and I signaled him to lather the Olds while he was at it. Then I limped across the wet floor and rode the elevator to my floor.

I hadn't really forgotten about Roxy Bolac. By now she could have given me up as an unreconstructed square and cut out for pads where the pot was greener. When I pushed open the door I realized I had sold her short by several miles.

She was there all right, and she had been busy rearranging my living room. Below the sofa she had dragged a mattress and covered it with a blanket from the bed. She was sitting on it cross-legged, a pair of bongo drums between her thighs, listening to Bird Parker soar through my Ampex. Her feet were bare and the only things between her and the air-conditioning were silky panties and a bra that was meeting a hard test. Beside her on the mattress stood a scotch bottle and a nearly empty glass. When she heard the door click shut her eyes opened lazily but her fingers didn't miss a beat.

Nodding at her, I walked over to the bar, opened a bottle and poured myself a slug. I must have needed it because it coasted down like milk and honey. I poured myself another, tossed most of it off and pulled off my coat.

As I unfastened the leather harness her eyes opened a little wider, but only for a moment. Then the remote, smoky look returned and I shoved the holstered pistol up on the closet shelf.

I loosened my tie and opened my collar. As I walked back to her I found that most of the pain had left me. Four ounces of scotch was as good as two demerols any night.

Settling down beside her, I leaned my shoulders back against the front of the sofa and lifted my glass. Her hair smelled as fresh and sweet as grass in an Easter basket. Her eyes studied me, utterly unashamed and utterly amoral. The tune ended and the room was suddenly quiet. The rim of. her glass tinkled against mine. We drank and I murmured, "Cozy."

"Crazy," she breathed.

"I'm home," I said. "Did you put the cat out, darling?"

"This cat's in to stay."

"Did you stoke the fire, sweetie pie?"

"Like frantic, lover."

"Did you leave a note for the milkman, pet?"

"He'll get the message, Daddy."

"Is Junior asleep, pumpkin?"

"Bathed, powdered and sleeping like a soldier, precious." She rubbed against me and nibbled the lobe of my ear. "But when he wakes up he'll be ready to go."

"Yes, baby," I said softly.

And then The Bird took over.

www.ingramcontent.com/pod-product-compliance
Lightning Source LLC
Chambersburg PA
CBHW030346180626
46812CB00007B/2775